PUFFIN BOOKS

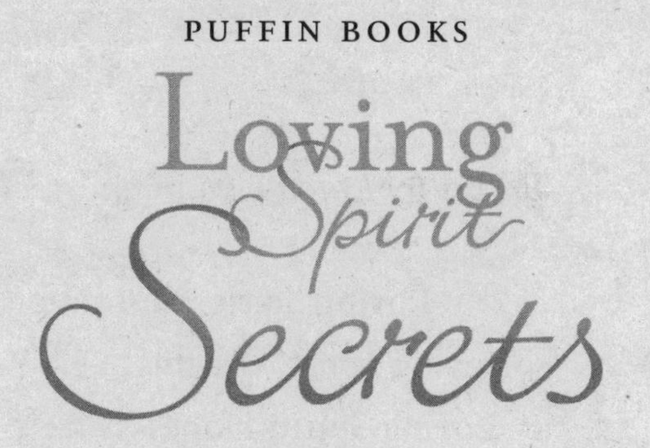

Linda Chapman lives in Leicestershire with her family and two dogs. When she is not writing, she spends her time looking after her three children, reading, talking to people about writing, and horse riding whenever she can.

You can find out more about Linda on her websites: *lindachapman.co.uk* and *lindachapmanauthor.co.uk*

Books by Linda Chapman

Loving Spirit

Loving Spirit: Dreams

Loving Spirit: Hopes

Loving Spirit: Secrets

PUFFIN

PUFFIN BOOKS

Published by the Penguin Group
Penguin Books Ltd, 80 Strand, London WC2R 0RL, England
Penguin Group (USA) Inc., 375 Hudson Street, New York, New York 10014, USA
Penguin Group (Canada), 90 Eglinton Avenue East, Suite 700, Toronto, Ontario, Canada M4P 2Y3
(a division of Pearson Penguin Canada Inc.)
Penguin Ireland, 25 St Stephen's Green, Dublin 2, Ireland (a division of Penguin Books Ltd)
Penguin Group (Australia), 250 Camberwell Road, Camberwell, Victoria 3124, Australia
(a division of Pearson Australia Group Pty Ltd)
Penguin Books India Pvt Ltd, 11 Community Centre, Panchsheel Park, New Delhi – 110 017, India
Penguin Group (NZ), 67 Apollo Drive, Rosedale, Auckland 0632, New Zealand
(a division of Pearson New Zealand Ltd)
Penguin Books (South Africa) (Pty) Ltd, 24 Sturdee Avenue, Rosebank,
Johannesburg 2196, South Africa

Penguin Books Ltd, Registered Offices: 80 Strand, London WC2R 0RL, England

puffinbooks.com

First published 2012
001 – 10 9 8 7 6 5 4 3 2 1

Set in Sabon Lt Std 12/16 pt
Typeset by Palimpsest Book Production Limited, Falkirk, Stirlingshire
Printed in Great Britain by Clays Ltd, St Ives plc

British Library Cataloguing in Publication Data
A CIP catalogue record for this book is available from the British Library

ISBN: 978–0–141–32835–5

www.greenpenguin.co.uk

To Ellie, Luke, Joe and Spirit –
this is your story and I am so glad I could tell it

Listen and I will speak
Ask and I will answer

Spirit . . .

Walking up the empty field bordered by grey stone walls, Ellie hummed softly to herself, the summer air warm on her bare arms. Behind her the sun had sunk down behind the mountains and the early evening sky was streaked with rose-pink light. It was peaceful in the field away from the bustle of the busy yard below, the shouting of her uncle as he gave lessons in the schooling ring, the clatter of hooves and the banter of the grooms. Out here in the field, the only sounds were the occasional baa from a sheep or a bird calling out overhead. Ellie felt excitement build inside her. Finally. The moment she'd been waiting for all day.

Her eyes fixed on the mound of earth ahead of her – Spirit's month-old grave. Ignoring the strain in her protesting legs, Ellie ran up the last bit of the slope and stopped. Small shoots of grass were already starting to push up through the sun-baked mound.

Shutting her eyes, Ellie focused on her breathing,

drawing in the clear air, letting it flow into the ground through the soles of her boots.

Spirit. She reached out with her mind, feeling for her horse's familiar energy, trying to connect with it. *Spirit? Are you there?*

Time seemed to stand still and then she heard a soft whicker.

Opening her eyes, she saw a grey horse standing on the hillside in the half-light. Her heart leapt as he started walking towards her, his ears pricked, his familiar eyes wise and true. He looked strong and healthy; the scars on his neck and shoulder had faded, and his ribs were well covered. As he came nearer, she could see the whirl of hair in the centre of his forehead, see the individual strands of his long forelock, the soft gleam of his white-grey coat.

Stopping in front of her, he reached out for her hands, the whiskers on his muzzle tickling her skin.

Ellie swallowed. Even though Spirit had appeared to her many times now, she always felt slightly dizzy with shock when it happened. Spirit was dead. His body had been buried in the grave a month ago, but here he was. When he appeared to her like this, she could see him, touch him, hug him, speak to him.

Her hands reached out, her fingers tracing wonderingly over his face. Putting her arms round his warm neck, she closed her eyes and buried her face in his soft mane. *I'm so glad you're here.* She didn't need to speak the words out loud; just as when he had been alive, he could hear her thoughts.

Spirit nuzzled her hair. *Always.*

Ellie felt the world fade away. Their love was so strong that even death couldn't part them.

Safe in their bubble of warmth and love, the girl and horse stood on the hillside, twilight darkening to night around them.

Chapter One

Ellie patted Gem, a blue roan hunter pony.

'You're such a good boy,' she murmured as she rode him back to the horsebox. 'You did so well today.'

A second-place rosette was tied to the string round her waist. Gem was only young and he could be nervous, but she'd been working hard with him and he'd performed really well just now in the ring in his first big open class. The show ground was buzzing – children were being mounted on to ponies, grooms putting the final polish on hooves and coats, parents talking into mobile phones, and horsebox ramps clattering as horses were led in and out. The July sun blazed down and Ellie felt hot in her show jacket and yellow jodhpurs.

It was only eleven thirty in the morning, but already she had competed in two show classes and had helped prepare three other horses. Her uncle, Len Carrington, owned a very successful hunter showing yard in north

Derbyshire and show days were always madly busy. More often than not the team would leave the yard at a very early hour of the morning with a string of horses and ponies, some owned by her uncle, others that he looked after and prepared for clients. Despite the early starts, Ellie loved show days. There was nothing to beat arriving at a new show ground just as the sun was rising in the sky, feeling the excitement at the day ahead, seeing horses and ponies being unloaded from lorries, greeting the other competitors. Now it was the summer holidays, there were shows every weekend and often in the week too. It was so different from her old life back in New Zealand. Ellie shook her head at the thought. A year ago she'd never even visited England and, although she had always ridden, she hadn't known anything about English horse and pony showing. Now it felt like her whole life.

'So how did you get on?' Sasha, the junior groom, came out of the lorry as Ellie rode Gem over. Sasha was carrying a rug, her make-up perfect as always, her blonde hair poker-straight.

Ellie showed her the blue rosette and dismounted. 'He was really good.'

'Excellent.' Sasha smiled.

When Ellie had first come to live at her uncle's yard, she and Sasha hadn't got on, but in recent weeks Sasha had seemed to thaw towards Ellie and was now quite friendly.

'I'll fetch his headcollar and wash him down,' the blonde girl offered. 'You get changed.'

'Thanks.' Ellie went up the steps into the living quarters. Her uncle's horsebox was one of the smartest on the show ground. It was glossy white and silver on the outside and the living quarters were like those of a very luxurious caravan. There were walnut cabinets, a leather sofa, a shower and two beds, one above the horses and one above the driver's cab. A sandy terrier was lying curled up on the sofa.

'Hey, Pip.' The little dog's stumpy tail thumped against the sofa, but the only person she would run to greet was her owner, Luke.

Ellie pulled on her jeans over her show jodhpurs, took off her jacket and shirt and put on a T-shirt, then shook her long, wavy, dark blonde hair free from the hairnet that kept it neatly in place.

She went back outside, checking her watch, wondering how everyone else from the yard was doing. Her uncle had three clients there that day – she knew he would be off with them, dealing with their horses.

'Luke should be getting Gabriel ready for the intermediate working hunter,' said Sasha. 'Have you seen him?'

Ellie shook her head. 'No, sorry.' Luke was her uncle's eighteen-year-old nephew from the other side of the family to her. He lived with them and worked full time on the yard.

Sasha rolled her eyes. 'Guess he's probably so busy chatting up some girl he's forgotten he has a class.' Ellie gave her a look. Sasha and Luke had been going out for a while, but they'd split up some weeks ago. Sasha had a new boyfriend now and Luke was going out with a girl called Anna Hallett. 'You know, I am *so* over Luke!' Sasha huffed. 'Rob treats me much better. Luke only cares about himself.'

She glanced at Ellie, inviting her to join in with criticizing Luke, but Ellie didn't. Tall and broad-shouldered, with dark hair and a mocking smile, Luke could be arrogant and very annoying, but Ellie knew there was another side to him too. When Spirit had been diagnosed with cancer and had to be put to sleep the previous month, Luke had been a rock of support. 'He's not that bad,' Ellie said.

Sasha raised her pencilled eyebrows. 'Really?'

Ellie sensed the older girl's prickliness but decided to avoid an argument. She shrugged. 'Look, I'll see if I can find him.'

She set off. As she walked round the horsebox she heard the sound of raised voices and clattering hooves and paused. None of those sounds was unusual on a show ground, but there was something this time that made her hesitate.

Help me!

The voice came clearly into her head. Ellie's gaze fell on a woman and teenage girl with a dapple-grey horse, just a few horseboxes away. Ellie had seen the people before but not with this particular horse. 'Lexi, stand still!' the girl was shouting, shaking the reins.

The grey mare pulled her head sharply back, her rear hooves clattering into the ramp again. Ellie could feel tension and pain pulsing off her.

'Stand still, you daft thing!' growled the square-set woman. Her hair was dyed blonde, cut short. Her tanned face had deep wrinkles.

'I don't know why you bought her, Mum!' the girl complained. 'She's a total nightmare. All she's done today is shake her head.'

'She just needs teaching some manners.' The woman yanked the reins hard.

The horse shot backwards, her eyes rolling, her ears flat back. *Help me!* her voice said again.

Ellie blinked. She had a special gift – an ability to communicate with horses – which meant she could hear what they were saying, ask them questions and understand their answers. Spirit had shown her how to use this ability. But she'd never had a horse speak to her first; she'd only ever heard them when she had asked them if they wanted to speak to her.

The grey tossed her head, stamping a front hoof in agitation. *Help me, help me, help me.*

Ellie realized that the mare wasn't talking specifically to her. She was just sending out a panicked message so strongly that Ellie was picking it up. She broke into a run.

'Stop it!' she exclaimed as the woman pulled on the horse's bridle again. 'Stop doing that!'

The woman and girl turned, surprise on their faces.

'It's OK, beautiful.' Ellie reached out her hand gently to the horse. The mare touched Ellie's fingers with her muzzle and instantly Ellie felt a pain sear across her own head behind her ears. She knew without question she was experiencing what the mare was feeling right then. 'She's in pain!'

The woman frowned, wrinkles deepening. 'And who the hell are you? A vet?'

'I just know she is!' Ellie said hotly. 'She's got a head injury. You've got to listen to me. You can't take her in the ring.'

'I think you'll find I can!' The woman's hard eyes narrowed. 'You're Ellie Carrington, aren't you? Len's niece?'

'You live with Luke Black?' the girl said, looking interested.

Ellie could only think about the mare. 'You mustn't ride her.'

'And you can mind your own flamin' business!' The woman pulled the mare round. 'Get changed, Katie. I'll find a martingale; that'll keep her head down.'

'Stop being so stupid – just listen to me!'

The woman glared. 'Who are you calling stupid?'

Ellie gave her an angry look. 'Well, if you won't listen and –'

'Ellie!' A hand closed on her arm. She swung round, her eyes travelling upwards and meeting Luke's blue gaze. His dark hair was falling over his forehead, his expression curious. 'What's going on here?'

'She's got a screw loose that's what's going on!' snorted the woman. 'Telling us we shouldn't ride our horse. That it's got a headache.'

'She's a *she*, not an it!' snapped Ellie. 'And I'm right! You shouldn't ride her today!'

Luke gave the woman an apologetic look, flicking his eyes towards Ellie. 'Sorry, we try to keep her under control, but sometimes the drugs wear off. Come on, Ellie.' He bundled her away. 'See you, Ann.'

'No!' Ellie tried to break free from him.

Luke responded by lifting her up and putting her over his shoulder in a fireman's lift.

'Luke!' Ellie struggled, thumping his shoulder furiously. 'Put me *down*!'

Luke strode a few horseboxes away and dumped her on the ground. 'Sure.'

The breath bumped out of her. 'You . . . you . . .' Ellie spluttered as she scrambled to her feet. 'Look, I have to stop them riding that horse!'

'Ellie!' Luke grabbed her arm and stopped her as

she tried to dodge past him. 'Whoa! Look, just wait a second. I don't know what's got into you, but you can't go round telling people not to ride their own horses.' He shook his head. 'Girl, you have seriously flipped!'

'I haven't! I just know there's something wrong with their mare. It's one of my feelings – you know the hunches that I get, Luke!' No one else knew she could talk to horses; they all thought that she worked out what was wrong with them because she had good intuition and horse sense. 'Maybe if I just spent some time with her I could help . . .' An idea sprang into Ellie's head and she grabbed Luke's hands, her tone changing. 'Luke, I've got it! Give me a distraction,' she wheedled.

'No.' He was shaking his head.

'Yes!' she insisted. 'You can do it. Just give me five minutes! Come on!' she pleaded, dragging him back to the box. Ann and her daughter were both in the living quarters now. The mare was tied up, still tossing her head. 'Just five minutes, please!'

Luke gave in just as she'd hoped. 'You're a nutjob, but go on then . . . you've got five minutes.'

'Thanks!'

Ellie saw him walk to the jockey door and knock on it. 'Hey, Katie,' he said as it opened. 'Just thought I'd come back and say hi.' He leant against the door frame, and from the tone of his voice Ellie could almost picture the disarming smile on his face. 'You and I haven't caught up for ages, and Ann, you're looking well. Sorry about Ellie just before. She can be a bit weird.' Ellie glared at his back but then focused on Lexi, who was watching her.

'Hey there.' Ellie went closer. Putting her hand on Lexi's neck, she caught her breath as the pain shot through her head again. It wasn't just the physical pain that made her wince. She could sense deep swirling emotions – unhappiness, panic, agitation. Often it took a while for a horse to open up and share its feelings, but she could feel the mare wanted help so much she was reaching out desperately, seeming to know that Ellie was able to understand her in a way no other human could.

Ellie's mind was flooded with images sent by Lexi as the mare tried to communicate. She saw the mare falling at a jump while doing a cross-country course, felt the injury to her neck, saw her afterwards when she resisted having a bridle put on . . .

No one knows. Lexi's voice echoed in Ellie's head. *Help me. Please.*

Aware that time was ticking away and that Luke wouldn't be able to keep Ann and Katie talking for long, Ellie made a decision. She couldn't do much. Lexi wasn't hers. But maybe she could help her a little. Just before Spirit had died she'd discovered that as well as being able to talk to horses, she could often help them feel better with her hands. She quickly focused her mind on healing. Her fingers tingled. When she did this, she felt as if she was a channel, allowing new energy to flow from outside her into the horse, easing pain. She moved a hand to Lexi's chest and the mare's head dropped, her back relaxing. Ellie touched Lexi's forehead lightly, sensing the mare's energy changing –

'What the ruddy hell do you think you're doing?' Ann Turner's voice snapped out.

The mare jerked her head up. Ellie swung round to see Ann and Katie both staring at her. Luke was spreading his hands apologetically.

'Get your hands off my flamin' horse! I'll be talking to your uncle about this!'

Ellie felt desperate. She'd done her best, hopefully given the mare some relief, but Lexi was still hurting. 'Please don't take her in the class,' she pleaded. 'She really has injured herself – you must have her checked by a vet.'

Ann went red with rage.

'And with that, I think we'll say goodbye,' said Luke hurriedly. Grabbing Ellie's shoulders, he steered her away.

'You didn't give me long enough!' Ellie protested.

'Gratitude please? I gave you five. What were you doing anyway?'

'Just trying to help. That horse is in pain.'

'From what Katie was saying she *is* a pain,' commented Luke. 'They haven't been able to put the bridle on her all week. I reckon they won't be keeping her.'

Ellie had an idea. 'We should get Uncle Len to buy her. She's lovely. She's injured – that's the only reason she's playing up. Will you help me persuade him? He'll listen to you more than me.'

'So, not only have I got you away from Ann and stopped her killing you and had to spend five minutes talking to her, you now want me to persuade Len to buy a horse? What's it worth?' His eyes teased her suddenly. 'A kiss?'

Ellie felt heat rush into her cheeks. 'I'll . . . I'll buy you a can of Coke.'

'Gee, now how can I refuse that?' Luke said dryly.

To Ellie's intense relief, they had reached the lorry and she ran the last few strides.

Sasha had Gabriel tacked up. 'Where have you been?'

Luke grinned. 'Aw, have you been missing me that much, Sash?'

Sasha shot him an unamused look. 'It's almost your class.'

'Then isn't it lucky I arrived just in time? Thanks for getting Gabe ready.' Luke grabbed his hat and took Gabriel's reins. The bright bay hunter nuzzled him affectionately. Luke glanced at Ellie. 'Now, do you think you can avoid getting into trouble for five minutes? Or am I likely to come back and find you've decided to pick a fight with half the show ground?'

Sasha looked curious. 'What?'

'Ask that headcase there!' said Luke cheerfully as Ellie glared at him. 'See you later. And, Ellie . . .'

'Yes?' she said warily.

'I still think a kiss would persuade me!'

Ellie's cheeks blazed as Sasha swung round and stared at her.

'Later!' With an infuriating grin, Luke rode away.

Chapter Two

After having to answer Sasha's curious questions and completely deny that there was anything going on with Luke, Ellie tacked up Barney, the next pony she was riding. It felt strange to get him ready. Her cousin Joe, Len's son, had always ridden him before, but Joe was now in Canada, working on a yard that specialized in natural horsemanship techniques.

'I know you miss him, don't you, boy?' Ellie said, patting Barney's liver-chestnut neck. 'Me too.' The pony picked up the bottom of her T-shirt in his teeth and pulled it up, exposing her tummy.

'Hey!' Ellie exclaimed, hastily pulling it down and checking no one had seen.

Barney snorted, sending a splatter of water droplets all over her.

'Barney!' Ellie could have sworn Barney winked. He was the cheekiest pony in the yard and if not watched would undo his stable door and the doors of the ponies around him, and let them all out. Ellie hoped he'd behave for her in the ring. 'You'd better!' she warned him.

Barney gave her a wounded look, as if to say, *Would I ever do anything else?*

Leaving him tied with a double knot, Ellie got changed and then rode him to the working-in area. He strode out, his ears pricked. He loved competing and had a brilliant jump. As a working hunter pony, Barney had to tackle a course of jumps and would be marked for how well he jumped them, as well as on the individual show where the judge marked his conformation and way of moving. The working hunter pony class was Ellie's favourite because it gave her the chance to jump. She loved showing, but she secretly dreamt of being a show jumper one day.

The aim that afternoon, though, was to qualify Barney for HOYS – the Horse of the Year show – which would take place in October. There were two big shows in the showing season: HOYS and the Royal International Horse show, which was on in a week's time. Barney had already qualified for the Royal International. As well as the class that day being a chance to qualify for HOYS, it was a practice run for the following week, although it hadn't been decided yet if Luke or Ellie would ride him. Ellie could feel the butterflies in her stomach. Barney had won so much in the last two years with Joe that if he went in the ring and didn't perform well today, it would be completely obvious she was to blame.

Ellie really missed Joe being on the yard. She sighed. There had been so many changes in the last year, leaving New Zealand for England when her parents were killed in a car accident; becoming best friends with Joe and then losing him when he was sent to Canada; buying Spirit and discovering her gift for communicating with animals, and then, last month, having to say goodbye to Spirit when he was put to sleep. That had seemed impossible to bear, but he had come back to her and she could talk to him still.

She and Barney started warming up. The working-in area was full of ponies and horses trotting and cantering around. Three jumps had been put up in the centre and people were taking it in turns to practise over them. Trainers watched with critical eyes, while grooms hurried about putting finishing touches to the ponies' coats. Ellie smiled at a few people and said hi. She knew most of the other riders now from the shows she had been in. Week after week she found herself facing the same people in the ring, and she was beginning to work out who was friendly, who wasn't, who she could chat with and who would ignore her.

Luke had told her that the week of the Royal International would be good fun. It was one of the few shows that Len stabled the ponies and horses at and Luke and Ellie would be staying there all week with the other show teams. It would make a change from the usual yard routine back at High Peak Stables and Ellie was really looking forward to it. Her very first international show. The only downside was that she'd be away from Spirit for the week.

Feeling Barney pulling eagerly at the bit, she let him trot on. When she was happy with how he was moving, she rode over to the ringside. The intermediate working hunter class was on and Luke was waiting by the ropes for his turn.

'How's it going?' Ellie got off for a few minutes to give Barney a break.

'Not a bad course. I'll walk it with you before you take Barney in. I'm right at the end of my class.'

'Do you need me to fetch Sasha?'

Each rider usually had a trainer or groom with them to help untack the horse after the individual show before they did the conformation section.

'It's all right, Len's coming over. He's in a good mood. Carey got the HOYS ticket on Alfie in her class and Melissa came third.'

'Oh, brilliant.' Carey Moss and Melissa Williams were two of Len's clients; they had horses who competed in the intermediate classes.

'He's schmoozing Veronica Armstrong at the moment, hoping she'll buy a new horse, I think.'

Ellie smiled wryly. Veronica Armstrong was a very rich client who owned quite a few of the horses on Len's yard, including two ponies her annoying children rode.

'Talking of new horses, there's that grey mare,' said Luke, nodding behind Ellie. Ellie looked round and saw Katie Turner riding over on Lexi. The mare had a tight martingale on that kept her head down. She was fighting against it, plunging round and shaking her head. People scattered out of the way as she came ricocheting across the collecting area.

'She's never going to jump, Mum!' Katie exclaimed.

'Make her!' Ann Turner snapped, her face looking more like a bulldog's than ever.

Katie brought Lexi to a halt. The mare fidgeted unhappily as she waited to enter the ring. The steward unclipped the rope, letting Katie in.

'Whoa!' said Luke as the mare leapt forward with a massive plunge.

Ellie could hardly bear to watch. She thought her healing had helped slightly, but there was no doubt in her mind the horse was in pain still. Katie moved her into a canter. Going forward round the ring, the mare seemed to settle down as Katie rode round the outside of the jumps, waiting for the signal to start.

Ellie bit her lip. She didn't have a good feeling about this. 'She's not going to jump.'

Just then a gruff voice snapped behind them. 'What

the hell are you doing, Luke? You're up next but one. Get Gabriel moving!'

Ellie and Luke saw the stocky figure of Len striding towards them.

Luke started backing Gabriel up.

Len caught sight of the grey mare in the ring. 'Nice-looking horse,' he commented, his grey-blue eyes narrowing assessingly in his weathered face.

'She belongs to the Turners. But I don't think they want to keep her. You should buy her,' Luke called as he started to circle Gabriel round the collecting ring.

The starting horn went and Katie cantered Lexi to the first fence. The mare's head shot up as she saw the jump, a panicked look on her face. Ellie knew if she tried to jump the pain would be really bad, particularly with the tight martingale holding her head down. Lexi seemed to sense this too. Reaching the jump she stopped, her back legs skidding underneath her. Katie fell forward on her neck.

Lifting her whip, she gave the mare three whacks and turned her round, hitting her again. But there was no way Lexi was jumping the fence. She refused again and again, pain in her eyes. On the third refusal, the horn went off and the horse was eliminated for stopping three times. She plunged her way out of the ring with Katie looking red-faced and furious.

Luke rode over. 'Told you, Len. Buy her. Ellie took

a look at her earlier and reckons she's just injured and can easily be sorted out.'

'That was a total embarrassment!' said Katie, riding over to her mother and dismounting. 'First fence elimination. I don't know why we ever bought her!'

Ellie could see the unhappiness on Lexi's face now she was out of the ring. 'Poor thing,' she whispered.

Len looked at her. 'So, you've got one of your hunches about that mare?'

She nodded.

Len eyes narrowed. Ellie wondered what he would do. There was no love lost between them, but she'd had too much success with her 'hunches' as he called them for him to completely dismiss what she said. 'Hey, Ann. Is that animal for sale?' he called. 'I'll buy it from you.'

'Will you now?' Ann Turner said belligerently.

Len wasn't fazed. 'Yes.' He named a figure. 'Well?'

'I paid twice that,' Ann replied, scowling.

'It's just been eliminated first fence. That's my only offer.' Len turned.

'No, wait!' Ann said hastily. 'OK. Done. You can take it with you today. The sooner we're shot of it, the better.'

Len went to the horse and looked her over. Ellie

saw the faintest of smiles flicker at the edges of his hard mouth. If Ellie was right that the mare was just injured and could be healed, he'd made a good bargain and he knew it.

Ann caught sight of Ellie and frowned. For a moment, Ellie thought she would say something to Len about what had happened earlier, but she seemed to decide not to. She'd got rid of the horse and seemed happy enough with that. Looking at the dapple-grey mare, Ellie felt her heart leap – she couldn't wait for a chance to communicate with her properly and hopefully really help her. But for now there were other things to think about. Luke rode up. It was almost his turn in the ring.

He halted Gabriel beside her and she instinctively checked the bay horse's girth.

'Thanks.' Luke looked supremely cool. Whereas most people were anxious before a class, Luke never seemed affected by nerves. He was in his element when competing, perfectly focused and with an innate understanding of how best to show a horse off, whether it was jumping or working on the flat.

Ellie wiped his long leather boots. 'Good luck.'

'Thanks. Can you check the bridle too?' When Luke was about to enter the ring, his usual flippancy dropped and he became serious and attentive to every detail – every speck of dust had to be removed, every bit of leather secured neatly and tidily. Ellie preferred him when he was like this, when he seemed to really care and not mind about showing it.

The steward released the rope to let him in.

Luke moved Gabriel forward, his body perfectly balanced in the saddle. Ellie couldn't help thinking of the contrast with Lexi. Whereas the mare had fought her rider, Gabriel had his ears pricked and was striding out.

'Go, Luke!' Ellie breathed as the starting horn went and Luke turned into the first jump. She needn't have worried. Luke maintained perfect control and Gabriel flew round the course at a steady gallop.

'Good riding,' Len said, nodding his head appreciatively as Luke and Gabriel cleared the fourth jump. Ellie knew he saw a lot of himself in Luke – his focus, determination and winning attitude. It was why he had taken an interest in him right from the start, when Luke was a young boy.

Luke was certainly riding a foot-perfect round. Gabriel was acting like the perfect hunter, eager but in control, his stride adjusting perfectly to meet the different fences. As they landed after the final fence with a clear round, Luke grinned and thumped Gabriel on the neck.

'Yes!' Ellie gave him a thumbs-up and he winked at her as he rode Gabriel into the next ring, where the second judge was waiting to watch Gabriel's individual show. Walk, trot, canter, gallop – Luke made Gabriel look as if he was an effortless ride. After that, Len helped him strip off the saddle and brush Gabriel down, then Luke completed the final phase of the class, walking and trotting Gabriel in hand. He led him out of the ring, patting him.

'Nice work, lad,' Len said approvingly.

'You did brilliantly!' Ellie said. Luke looked pleased.

Len and Luke quickly saddled up the bay. Luke had been the last to ride in the class and the results were soon announced. The loudspeaker crackled into life: 'First: 135, Luke Black riding Len Carrington's Highcross Gabriel.'

Len nodded in satisfaction. 'Right, I'd better get back to the others,' he said. 'But I'll be here when you take Barney in. Don't let him stand around too long.'

He strode away. Ellie watched in delight as Luke was presented with the winner's rosette. Another qualification for HOYS. It was turning into an excellent day for the yard!

Luke led the lap of honour and galloped out. He brought Gabriel to a halt and jumped off, sweeping Ellie into a hug.

'Well done!' She hugged him back, sharing his elation. As he released her, his eyes caught hers. For a moment, Ellie felt a click, a connection, almost like when she communicated with a horse, and she was suddenly very aware of the feel of his arms round her. Feeling disconcerted, she stepped quickly away. 'Uncle Len's bought that mare. We'll be taking it home with us,' she gabbled.

'Excellent. Will you be able to do your –' Luke grinned – '*thing* with her?'

Ellie took a breath, trying to feel normal. Luke didn't seem to have felt anything out of the ordinary just now, but for some reason she was finding it hard to focus, still feeling the imprint of his arms round her. *Stop being stupid*, she told herself. *You can't like Luke in* that *way. You mustn't.* Not only was he already going out with someone and incapable of being faithful, but he had the ability to really irritate her a lot of the time.

'I'll try,' she answered.

'Cool.' Luke stretched. 'Well, I'd better take Gabe back to the lorry.' But just then a pretty girl with red hair and a tight chocolate-brown T-shirt walked past him on her way to the nearby coffee stall. Luke looked her up and down. 'On second thoughts maybe I could do with a coffee first,' he said, setting off after her.

'Luke!' Ellie exclaimed.

He looked round in surprise. 'What?'

Ellie felt a stab of irritation. 'I thought you were supposed to be going out with Anna.'

'I am, but . . .' He hesitated and then headed after

the girl again. 'It's a shame to deprive all the other girls in the world!' He grinned. 'I'm just going to offer to buy her a coffee, Ellie. Loosen up.'

She watched as he led Gabriel after the girl. 'Hey there.'

The girl turned in irritation, but as she took in Luke and clocked his handsome face, the annoyance turned to a smile. 'Hi. Can I help you?'

'My horse saw you passing and wanted to say hello.' Luke turned to Gabriel and spoke to him. 'See, I told you she'd be too busy to stop. Now you've embarrassed me.'

The girl looked amused. 'He's lovely.' She patted Gabriel, slanting Luke a look through her eyelashes. 'Really lovely.'

'He's not the only one,' said Luke. The girl raised her eyebrows at the corniness. Luke grinned and nodded to a grey horse behind the girl. 'Look behind you – that hunter over there is just gorgeous.'

The girl giggled. 'Are you getting a coffee?'

'Oh, yes,' said Luke, his smile matching hers. 'Can I buy you one too?'

'OK. Thanks.'

Ellie rolled her eyes. Honestly! Luke was useless at being faithful. She'd thought he might manage it with Anna Hallett. Anna was very beautiful – the daughter of one of Len's main sponsors and clients. So far she'd seemed to be keeping Luke on his toes.

Hang on, what's it to you what Luke does? she thought. *It's none of your business.*

But despite her sensible words, she couldn't stop herself feeling irritated and cross as she rode Barney away.

Chapter Three

Ellie lay on the sofa in the lorry, stroking Pip and listening to her iPod as her uncle drove home after the show. Barney had gone well in his class and been placed second, but Ellie's joy had been slightly dimmed by the fact that, straight afterwards, a man had approached Len to discuss buying Barney for his daughter.

A deal hadn't been finalized, but the man had made a generous offer and had arranged to visit the yard to try Barney out in a few days' time. Ellie knew that buying and selling was part of her uncle's business, but it was the first time that a pony she'd grown attached to at the yard might be sold.

She tried not to think about it, reminding herself of the new mare who was now in the back with the others. If horses and ponies weren't sold, then new horses like Lexi couldn't be bought. And maybe it would be best for Barney anyway – she knew he was the type of pony that needed to feel he had one special person who loved him, and she was so busy she didn't have time to give him all the attention he needed now Joe had gone. He might be happier in a new home.

She glanced at the other end of the sofa where Sasha was giggling and teasing as she chatted to her boyfriend, Rob, on her mobile phone. Luke had gone ahead of them on his motorbike. Sasha shrieked with laughter and Ellie shut her eyes and lay back, turning the volume up, her thoughts turning to Joe. It was at times like this that she missed him most. If he'd been there they would have been chatting about the show or the music they were listening to, or talking about the ponies and what he'd been reading about horses in his books. Ellie thought of his smiling greeny-grey eyes and tousled sandy-brown hair. He was her best friend. For a while she had wanted them to be more than friends, but Joe had felt there were too many problems because they were cousins. Ellie realized now that it had probably been the right choice, but she did miss having Joe there as a friend to share things with. *I'll email him when I get back*, she thought wistfully. *See how he's doing.*

At least she still had Spirit. She smiled as she pictured the grey horse, his ears pricked, his dark eyes full of love. She would see him soon. Happiness rose up inside her at the thought.

*

It was early evening when they returned. The tops of the mountains rose up behind High Peak Stables, their green slopes dotted with black-faced sheep, the sun sinking down towards them. Creamy heads of cow parsley edged the grass verges at the side of the car park, nodding in the gentle breeze. Ellie stretched after the drive. It had been a long day, but thankfully the show hadn't been too far from home. Inside the horsebox one of the horses stamped a hoof impatiently. Stuart and Helen, the two other grooms, came down from the yard to help as Len lowered the ramp. The new horse was nearest the exit. She saw Ellie and whinnied.

'So this is the new one?' said Stuart. He was an ex-jockey and had been working as Len's yard manager for the last ten years. Helen was his girlfriend. Len had rung him from the show to tell him to prepare a stable for the mare.

Len nodded. 'Should be a good working hunter if we can get her sorted out. She's a looker all right.'

'I'll take her in,' offered Ellie. 'She's called Lexi,' she said to Stuart and Helen, knowing her uncle wouldn't be bothered with things like the horse's name.

'Stick her in the barn next to Solo,' instructed Len.

Ellie nodded. Even just leading Lexi down the ramp she could feel an unhappy, anxious energy around the mare and she was longing for a chance to work with her. As she put her into the stall in the barn, the mare pushed against her as if asking her to help. 'I'll come back as soon as it's quiet,' Ellie promised. It would mean putting off seeing Spirit, but she knew that he'd want her to help Lexi.

Hurrying back to the car park, she helped unload the rest of the horses and ponies. As she led Gem into the pony barn, with Pip dancing around her feet, there was a shrill whinny and a tiny chestnut nose poked up over the stall door next to Gem's. Ellie smiled as Gem reached over the door and touched noses with the chestnut filly inside.

Hope, the little filly, had been orphaned a month ago. For a while it seemed that she wouldn't survive – she had refused to eat or drink after her mother had died, but Spirit had urged Ellie to talk to her and help heal her. He had also told her to let Gem and the foal go out in the field together. The two horses had instantly bonded and now hated being separated. Ellie watched Gem, whickering like an anxious mother as he snuffled Hope's pale, sticking-up mane and touched noses with her. Ellie let them have their reunion and then put Gem in the stall next door. 'You can go out in the field together tomorrow,' she said as she put on his lightweight stable sheet for the night.

Fastening the bolt on his stable door, she let herself into the filly's stall. The little foal was capricious and demanding but utterly cute. Ellie adored her. Hope pushed her tiny muzzle against her, eager for attention and love. Ellie rubbed her neck and felt a connection instantly open between them. It was strange with Hope. Whereas most horses had layers of memories and emotions and she often felt overwhelmed by them, the foal had only a few memories and when Ellie connected with her she just felt very intense simple emotions – love, excitement, anger . . .

Happiness radiated from the foal. Ellie could feel how much she liked being stroked and fussed. She wished she could stay in the stall, but she knew she should go and help with the other horses. Ellie sighed and reluctantly went to the door.

The filly put her ears back and nipped crossly at Ellie's arm.

'No, Hope!' Ellie chided.

The foal turned her back on her and sulked as if she felt she was being deserted.

Going back on to the yard Ellie found that Carey Moss had just returned from the show with the three intermediates in her horsebox, so there was more unloading and sorting out to be done. At last all the horses were settled for the night. The grooms had left and Len had gone into the house. Luke had apparently been home but had changed and gone straight out again for the evening. Ellie had never met anyone with such energy. He worked hard all day and then went out in the evening, often not returning until after midnight, but he never seemed tired or bad-tempered in the morning and was always on the yard at 7 a.m., joking and striding about, letting Len's ill humour slide off him.

Ellie headed to Lexi's stall. There were two barns at High Peak Stables, one for the ponies and one for the youngsters and liveries, as well as a courtyard with ten stables around it, a wash-stall, tackroom, rug store and feedroom. Len demanded neatness and everything was perfectly ordered and tidy. Leather headcollars hung outside each stable, leadropes clipped on and neatly coiled. Brooms and shovels were stacked against walls. Rugs were folded. Flower baskets hung from metal hooks, the bright summer blooms pruned and watered.

Lexi was pacing round in her stall, looking agitated. Catching sight of Ellie, she snorted.

'Shh. It's OK,' Ellie said soothingly as she let herself into the stable. Lexi came to her and pushed her head against her.

Ellie breathed in and out, focusing on the mare. She felt the connection open between them, like a door swinging back and she saw the same memory she'd seen before – the mare taking a cross-country jump, catching her front legs, somersaulting over, crashing down, the rider thrown clear. She felt a stabbing pain around her ears, the mare's pain becoming her own just as it had done earlier.

I tried to tell them how much it hurt, Lexi's thoughts came to her. Ellie saw images of her shaking her head and felt the longing for understanding, the desire for someone to listen. She saw the bridle being put on, yanked down when Lexi threw her head up. *Help me.*

Of course, Ellie promised her. *Now you're here you'll be OK. We'll make you better and when you're ready to be ridden again, I'll make sure you're ridden gently.*

She felt Lexi's gratitude and touched the mare's forehead. She concentrated on letting healing energy flow through her fingers. She knew she wouldn't be able to cure the physical pain completely, but she would try to ease it and get her uncle to call the vet the next day. Lexi's eyelids fluttered. Ellie worked her way round Lexi's body, touching the mare at different points, feeling the energy vibrating under her fingers, smoothing it, waiting to feel the energy flowing normally before moving on to the next spot. Finally, she reached Lexi's head again. The horse sighed deeply and Ellie felt a new sense of peace in her. The pain was still there, but it had lessened and, more importantly, Lexi now felt that someone understood.

Thank you for letting me help you, Ellie told the horse.

Stepping back, she felt the connection between

them close and she let herself out of the stable. She felt tired and energized at the same time. Talking to horses, healing them, took a lot of effort and concentration but left her feeling elated and she loved it. As she passed the other horses in their stalls, she stopped to pat each one. Those she had worked with before came to their doors eagerly. She stroked them, then finally left the barn and headed up to the fields.

Ten minutes later, Ellie was standing beside Spirit. The sun had set and the night was closing in. The woods that edged on to his field were dark with shadows. Wrapping her arms round his solid neck, Ellie felt a rush of emotions, happiness and sadness combined. Sadness that he would never be on the yard, like a normal horse again, a horse she could just open a stable door and see. Happiness that he was there and she could still talk to him and touch him. If she went to his grave to talk to him in the day, he would stay invisible although she could sense his presence and hear his voice, but when it was dark and no one could see them from the yard, he would appear to her, solid and warm, looking just as he had when he was alive only healthier and stronger. *Things haven't really changed*, she told herself. *I just have to come out here to see him in the evenings. He's still mine and we can still be together.* The more she told herself that, the more she believed it.

Shutting her eyes, she now rested her forehead against his neck.

You're tired. She heard Spirit's concerned voice in her mind.

She nodded. *It's been a long day.*

Let's go into the woods. I want to hear about it.

Ellie vaulted on to his back. Wrapping her hands in his mane, she felt her tiredness drain away and a new energy fill her.

The stone wall was ahead of them. Spirit broke into a trot and then a canter. Ellie felt his muscles gather and he lifted into the air. He cleared the wall easily before landing on the soft ground on the other side. She smiled as they slowed to a walk and started to wind their way through the trees. Ellie breathed in the scent of leaf mould as Spirit picked his way around the tree roots, branches cracking under his hooves.

So, what happened today?

Ellie told him all about the show – about the classes, about Luke, about Lexi. She felt Spirit's approval as she explained how she'd been to the mare that evening, talked to her and given her as much healing as she could.

You have a gift. She will feel much better.

I wish I could have made you better, Ellie thought.

Some damage can't be healed, Spirit replied softly. *You know that. And you did make me feel better. The end was better because you were there.*

Ellie felt tears sting her eyes. She didn't want to remember that time. It had been so black.

I'm glad you came back to me and we're together still, she said. *That nothing's really changed.*

Spirit snorted in agreement.

Where . . . where would you have gone? Ellie asked curiously a few moments later.

Spirit sent a picture to her mind of him standing on a beach in front of a rippling silver sea. On the far side was a distant land. He was staring towards it and she could feel the pull across the water, but as she watched him standing there, he turned and walked back towards her.

Ellie's fingers played in his soft mane. She could feel the contentment coming from him that he was here with her now. But did he wish he'd gone to that land? Did –

Walk in the present. Spirit's voice gently interrupted her thoughts.

Ellie sighed. He was right. He'd taught her once before that horses walk in the present, not worrying about the future or clinging to the past. It was a good way to be. She was here with him now. That was all that mattered. They carried on happily through the trees as the shadows darkened and the night birds started to call.

Chapter Four

Ellie went into the grey stone farmhouse and found Len in the kitchen, taking a beer from the fridge. The kitchen in the farmhouse was large with an old pine table. The window ledges were covered with an assortment of horse and motorbike magazines. Bags of feed supplements, boxes of crisps and crates of beer were piled up in one corner. The door to the lounge was open and through it Ellie could see the threadbare sofa and large TV. The house was fairly tidy but in no way as pristine as the yard.

She took off her boots, feeling the silence hanging heavy in the air. She rarely spoke to her uncle unless she had to.

Len flicked the bottle top off, using the opener attached to the draining board. 'Where have you been?'

'Just outside.'

'It's dark.'

Ellie shrugged.

Len's grey eyes narrowed. 'You've been moping over that grave again, haven't you?'

Ellie prickled. 'I've just been outside,' she said, trying to keep her voice level.

Len snorted. 'That bloody horse of yours is dead. You'd better toughen up, lass!' He laughed and threw the bottle cap into the rubbish. 'You're soft in the head.' He marched through to the lounge to watch TV.

Ellie bit back the retort that jumped to her lips. Her uncle had as much sensitivity as a bulldozer. She wanted to go up to her room but first she knew she had to tackle him about Lexi. She went to the doorway. 'The new horse. Lexi . . .'

'The grey mare?'

'Lexi,' said Ellie with a nod. 'I think she needs to see a vet. I think she's hurt her neck, behind her ears.'

Her uncle nodded but to her relief didn't challenge her. 'Fine. I'll ring John in the morning.' He picked up the remote control and turned the sound up. It was clear the conversation was over.

Ellie escaped thankfully upstairs. Her room was on the top floor. Shutting the door behind her, she went to the window and tried not to feel too lonely.

'Get him moving forward! You're riding like a sack of bloody potatoes!'

Len's voice rang in Ellie's ears the next day. She

could feel the sweat prickling in her hair under her hat and soaking through the back of her blue T-shirt. It was almost lunchtime and the sun was blazing down. Picasso, the dark bay working hunter pony she was riding, was having one of his days where he seemed determined to throw her off. He'd started by sidling and shying and then had a massive bucking fit, dumping her on the ground. She could tell there was nothing wrong with him; he was just in the mood for playing up. He was the most beautiful pony and stunning in the ring, but he was highly strung and temperamental. Ellie had bonded with him and he had days now where he would nuzzle her and show some affection, but on other days the devil just seemed to be inside him and he would throw diva-like tantrums for no reason at all.

'Forward!' barked Len. Ellie used her legs so hard that Picasso plunged to one side. She was ready for him, though, and moved with him, pulling his head up, circling him round. If only it wasn't so hot. There wasn't a breath of air and she could feel the heat rising from Picasso's dark coat. Her legs were aching and her hands damp with sweat.

'Rising trot! Work him on!' Picasso started to settle into a steadier trot, arching his neck as he admired his shadow on the ground. At the other end of the school, Luke was riding Troy, a large working hunter. As she passed, he teasingly held the reins in one hand

and brought Troy from a canter to a smooth halt, as if showing off how easily it could be done.

Ellie glared. Troy was a gentle, affectionate horse, always eager to please. Totally different from Picasso.

Luke just grinned infuriatingly at her.

Len dragged out four low jumps. 'Get rid of your stirrups,' he ordered Ellie. 'You too, Luke. You can join in with that bay.'

Troy! Ellie snapped in her head. She hated it when her uncle didn't use the horses' names. It seemed so disrespectful, as if they were just machines to him.

Bringing Picasso to a halt, she crossed her stirrups, her heart sinking. Even on a good day, Picasso had a tendency to buck when he first started jumping. She had a feeling she'd be hitting the floor again.

She was right. As she set off over the jumps, Picasso went faster and faster, and without her stirrups Ellie slipped in the saddle and lost her balance. When Picasso landed after the final jump, he threw his head down and bucked mischievously. She flew through the air and thudded into the sand.

Len swore. Catching Picasso, he brought him back over as Ellie got to her feet, slightly bruised and fed up, but not badly hurt. 'That'll teach you not to lose contact!' Len said.

Well, thanks for worrying if I'm all right, Ellie muttered to herself. She met her uncle's flint-like eyes and vaulted back on.

'Do it again. Do it right!' he said brusquely.

Ellie rode Picasso at the fences again. This time she stayed balanced and kept the contact, so was ready when he bucked at the end.

Her uncle gave a brief nod of approval.

He turned to Luke, who managed the fences perfectly on Troy, keeping in perfect balance with the horse and making it look easy.

'Nice work,' Len commented.

He made them ride over the fences again and again, varying the distances between jumps until he was happy with the way Troy and Picasso were going. 'Right, take those animals up the lane.' Opening the gate, he marched back down to the yard.

'Animals!' Ellie exclaimed as she and Luke rode out. 'Sometimes I think he would be just as happy with a business showing cars or tractors!'

'I know what you mean,' Luke agreed, letting Troy walk out on a loose rein. 'The horses have always been a business to Len, but he used to enjoy being around them before – at least he seemed to. I don't know when I last saw him ride just for pleasure, or even spend some time with a horse though.'

Ellie scowled. 'He drives me mad!'

Luke gave her a sympathetic look. 'It'll be better when you can drive. Then you'll have some independence and won't be stuck here all the time.'

'Great,' Ellie groaned. 'That's only two years and a few days away.'

'Of course – it's your birthday next week, isn't it?' Luke realized.

'Thursday,' said Ellie.

'We'll be at Hickstead. We'll have to celebrate in style.' Luke chuckled. 'Well, if you've managed not to end up in hospital by then. Picasso really had it in for you today.'

'I know! I wish Len was thinking of selling *him*, not Barney!' Ellie patted Picasso's neck to show she was only joking. 'I'll really miss Barney if he leaves,' she went on, her thoughts turning to the chestnut pony. 'I wish none of the horses ever had to be sold.'

'It's the way it is here,' said Luke. 'Don't become too attached to them. If you're going to be attached, get a horse of your own.'

Ellie frowned. 'Why don't you have your own horse?' She'd never really thought about it much, but suddenly she realized it was strange. It wasn't about money – Luke's parents were rich. Even though they had very little time for him, surely they would buy him a horse if he wanted one? She knew he'd loved the ponies he owned when he was younger because she'd seen how upset he'd been when he talked about two of them being put down.

Luke shrugged. 'Guess I don't want one.'

'But why not?'

'They break your heart.'

'That's no reason for not having a horse!' Ellie protested.

'Isn't it?' He gave her a look.

'No!' The pain Ellie had felt when Spirit died had been immense, utterly devastating, but she knew she would suffer that a million times rather than having lived without knowing and loving him. 'You can't live your life not loving just because you're afraid of getting hurt!'

'Looks like I can.' Luke started to whistle annoyingly.

'Luke!' Ellie felt anger rise inside her. She *knew* he wasn't as cold as he was making out. Why did he have to put on an act? 'You *don't* think like that. I don't believe you do.'

His voice was light. 'Believe it.'

'Well, if it's true, you're a coward!'

A muscle jumped in Luke's jaw. 'Thanks.'

The sensible part of Ellie's brain told her to just let it go – it was Luke's life and he could live it as he wanted. But the rest of her seethed with frustration. She stared straight ahead at Picasso's ears, hating him for saying what he had.

They didn't speak for a while.

It was Luke who eventually broke the silence. 'You know, *you* should buy another horse,' he said suddenly.

'What?' Ellie was so surprised she forgot her bad mood for a moment.

'I've been thinking about it.' The angry look on his face faded. 'It would be good for you. Why don't you get one? You really should.'

Ellie stared at him, taken aback by his change of mood. But seeing the genuine interest in his eyes, she let herself consider the idea. For a moment, she imagined it, a horse that was just hers – one that no one could sell or take away. A horse she could do whatever she liked with. No. She felt suddenly disloyal. She didn't need another horse; she had Spirit still.

'Well?' Luke pushed.

'I don't need a horse. I . . . I haven't got time for one,' she said quickly. 'There are so many ponies to ride with Joe gone.'

'So get a youngster.' Luke waved his hand in the air, bulldozing the obstacles away. 'I know. Buy the foal – buy Hope!'

'Hope?' Ellie echoed in surprise.

'Yeah! It would be perfect. I can't believe you haven't thought of it before. She's a looker and bred for jumping. She should make about 15.2 hands high when she's full grown, perfect for you. You could bring her on, do what you wanted with her, start riding her in a few years' time. Maybe show jump her. You two have a real bond, anyone can see that, and it would mean you'd have your own horse for now but not one that would take up riding time. I reckon Len's going to sell her soon; he only bought her because he wanted her mother. So why not do it?'

Ellie's head spun. The thought of buying the foal filled her with delight partly because it was such a mad, unexpected idea! But why not? Her parents had left her money in their will. Her gran was one of the people in charge of it, but she'd always said that Ellie could have money for anything reasonable – she'd let her buy Spirit. Surely she'd let her buy a foal. And Ellie hated the thought of Hope being sold on. 'I could, couldn't I?'

'Yeah!' Luke grinned at her, seeming to have forgotten all the earlier tension. 'Go for it, girl!'

'OK, I will!' Ellie declared. ' I'll ask Uncle Len when we get back!'

The yard was bustling when Ellie and Luke returned. Sasha and Helen were grooming while Stuart swept the yard. Horses looked over the loose-box doors around the courtyard, their coats gleaming, ears pricked. Carey and Melissa were riding their horses in the schooling ring.

Ellie washed Picasso down, then put him in his stable to dry off. She went to the office to see if her uncle was there. As she approached, she hesitated. If she planned to ask about buying the foal, she wanted to catch him in a good mood and he certainly hadn't been in one that morning. But just then the office door opened and Len came out, smiling.

'Hey, Stu,' he called across the yard. 'I've just had a phone call from Jeff Hallett. Get the box next to Starlight ready. A new horse is coming this afternoon.'

'What horse?' Stuart asked.

'Jeff's bought a new hack for his daughter. It's a youngster. Anna wanted a baby to bring on next season. It's just been backed apparently. A gelding, 15.1 hands high. Sired by Golden Glory.'

Stuart gave an appreciative nod. Golden Glory had been a champion hack who had won at the Horse of the Year show. 'Sounds interesting.'

'It's arriving later and Anna's coming for a lesson on Lucifer beforehand. Will you get him ready?'

'I'll do it,' Ellie offered.

Lucifer was a beautiful but difficult horse that Luke rode in the hack classes when Anna Hallett couldn't. The horse had a troubled past, but he trusted Ellie. It was very important he did well in shows. Jeff Hallett owned the horse-food company that sponsored Len, providing free food for all the horses on the yard.

Len nodded. 'Make sure he's groomed up really well, lass.'

'Sure. Uncle Len, can I ask you something first?' Ellie looked at her uncle's face. For once he looked almost jovial. 'You know Hope – the foal. What are you planning to do with her?' She held her breath.

‘I’ll sell her on. Why?’

‘Well . . .’ Ellie looked at him hopefully. ‘If Gran will let me, could I buy her from you?’

‘You?’

Ellie nodded.

‘Why would *you* want a foal?’

To love, to care for, to be mine . . . Ellie knew she couldn’t say that to him. ‘To bring on. I’ll work with her. Back her when she’s old enough. Sell her on in the end.’ She had no intention of selling the foal, but she knew she needed to speak a language her uncle understood.

‘So you want to see if you can make some money from her?’

Ellie nodded.

‘All right.’ Len nodded approvingly. ‘It’s a good attitude. You can buy her. See what you can do with her. We’ll do the same deal as we had with that grey you picked up at the sale. You can have her feed and stabling for free in return for the work you do for me.’

He walked back into the office. Ellie stood, rooted to the spot for a moment as it slowly dawned on her that this wasn’t just a mad plan any more – she was actually buying Hope if her gran agreed. She couldn’t wait to tell Spirit! It would be just like having him on the yard all over again. Her own horse there to love, who would love her back.

‘Well?’ Luke came over, Pip trotting at his heels. ‘What did he say?’

‘He said yes!’ Ellie grinned and bent down to ruffle Pip’s ears in delight.

‘Awesome!’ Luke said, pleased.

‘I want to go and see her.’

Ellie and Luke went to the field where Hope and Gem were turned out together. They were grazing, nose by nose.

‘She is a beauty,’ said Luke appreciatively.

Ellie nodded, taking in the filly’s pretty head, her intelligent, slightly stubborn eyes, her clean long limbs and strong back.

‘Better move on,’ said Luke, hearing a shout from the yard. He nudged her. ‘I’ll leave you with *your* horse.’ Giving a whistle to Pip who was nosing in the hedgerow, he walked away.

My horse. Ellie climbed over the gate. Gem and Hope came over. Touching Hope’s neck, Ellie was struck again at how simple the energy around the foal felt. There was no hidden pain, no deep anguish or difficult memories. Ellie felt suddenly awed. It was up to her to make sure Hope stayed happy, that the filly never had any bad memories that Ellie could possibly prevent.

‘I will look after you,’ she promised the filly. ‘For always.’

Remembering she’d made that promise once

before, her excitement faded a few notches. Owning Hope would be great, but Spirit was still with her and would always be her real horse – the one she loved most. She mustn't forget that.

She turned and looked up the slope to the field where his grave was. *Always and ever*, she thought.

Chapter Five

Anna Hallett arrived in her silver sports car. Shaking back her mane of dark brown hair, she waved at Luke as she walked up the yard, her tight cream breeches and short-sleeved T-shirt showing off her perfect figure. Ellie looked down at her own blue jodhpurs, dusty from her falls that morning, and T-shirt covered with slobber where Picasso had rubbed his mouth against her when she had taken off his bridle. Her long ponytail had shavings in it and she could tell she had a spot coming on her chin. She couldn't ever imagine looking so effortlessly glamorous and beautiful.

Luke went to meet Anna, Pip trotting beside him. Even in his work clothes he looked gorgeous too. They looked as if they should be in an advert together. Anna smiled up at Luke through her long eyelashes. 'Been missing me?'

'You bet,' he murmured.

Pip went over to greet Anna, putting her front

paws up on Anna's breeches. 'Get down!' Anna snapped, frowning.

Ellie went to the tackroom and fetched Lucifer's saddle and bridle. She knew Anna wouldn't want to tack him up herself but would expect him warmed up, ready and waiting in the school for her lesson with Len.

When Lucifer saw her coming, he pricked his ears and whinnied. Ellie smiled. Lucifer's dark eyes fixed on her.

'Hey, boy,' she said, letting herself into his stable. He nuzzled her. She pictured him when he'd arrived at the yard, attacking other horses, refusing human contact, threatening people who came into his stable with his teeth and hooves until Ellie had helped him. Feeling his lips hopefully exploring the outside of her pockets for treats, Ellie rubbed his neck.

She took Lucifer up to the schooling ring and rode him round, warming him up and enjoying the way he responded to the lightest of pressure on the reins. Lucifer liked to be trusted and the softer his rider was with their aids, the better he went.

When Anna came to the gate with Luke, Ellie halted. Most of Len's clients would smile and say thanks if Ellie had been working their horse in, but Anna didn't say a word to her.

'He's looking well,' Anna said to Luke.

'Ellie's in charge of grooming him and we ride him between us when you're not here,' Luke replied.

Anna's eyes barely flickered in Ellie's direction. 'Have you heard about my new horse?' she asked Luke as she went into the school.

'Yeah.'

Anna nodded. 'I want a youngster I can really work with. You know, one that I can feel I've brought on.'

Ellie stared. Anna didn't have a clue what it meant to bring a horse on. There was so much more to it than turning up and riding them occasionally. 'So are you going to come down every day then?' she said, dismounting.

Anna looked as startled as if the fence post had just talked. 'Sorry?'

'Well, that's what people do when they're bringing a young horse on. They work closely with them – every day.'

Anna gave a high laugh. 'I won't exactly be doing *that*!'

'Well then, you can't say you're –'

'Hey, Ellie,' Luke interrupted. 'Wasn't that Stu calling for you?'

She frowned. 'No.'

'I think it was,' he said firmly. 'Why don't you work Lucifer in, Anna? Len will be up in a moment and I'll just go with Ellie to see what Stu wants.'

Anna smiled at him. 'Come back soon, though.'

''Course,' he replied and winked at her. Then, grabbing Ellie's shoulder, he steered her out of the school.

'What are you doing?' she said, shaking him off as they walked through the gate.

'El-*liee*!' Luke stared at her. 'You can't go around offending one of Len's most important clients. You have to be nice to Anna.'

'So is that why you're going out with her?' retorted Ellie, unable to resist.

'No!'

'So how would she feel about you flirting with other girls like that girl at the show!'

'Don't you dare tell her about that!' Luke said warningly.

Ellie put her hands on her hips. 'Oh, you're *daring* me, are you?'

'No! Look, OK, you're right.' Luke took a deep breath, appearing to force himself to calm down. 'I shouldn't have chatted up that girl. But you shouldn't tell Anna that she doesn't know how to bring a young horse on. Agreed?'

Staring into his blue eyes, Ellie felt her anger fade slightly. It was a fair point, even she had to admit it. 'OK,' she muttered.

'Luke! What are you doing?' Anna called, a slight edge to her voice.

They looked round and saw she had halted and was watching them. 'Just coming. Stu doesn't need me after all.' Luke jumped back over the gate. 'So, come on then. Let me see how well he goes for you.'

Shaking her head, Ellie walked away down the yard.

Later that day, after Anna had left, John, the vet, arrived to examine Lexi. He diagnosed the mare as having a vertebra knocked out of place at the top of her spine, with muscle pain, advising a course of anti-inflammatories and visits from the equine physiotherapist. 'She'll be in pain until this injury is sorted out, so no exercise until the swelling and pain has gone,' he told Stuart and Ellie. 'Be very careful even putting a headcollar on. She looks like she'll be a really nice horse when she's better though.'

Ellie stroked the mare's cheek. 'We'll help you get well,' she promised as she took her headcollar off.

She wondered when the Halletts' new horse was arriving. Len had said it would be that afternoon.

She'd left the stable and found Luke pacing around the yard, talking angrily on his mobile. 'What? But why? Look, there's no need. I'm sure you're busy as always. Well, so what if Dad wants to come?' He broke off with a muttered exclamation. 'Whatever. Come if you must.' Clicking the END CALL button, he raised his eyes to the sky.

'What's up?' said Ellie, surprised at seeing Luke so tense. Usually, nothing ever fazed him.

'It's my parents. For some reason they've decided they're coming to Hickstead to watch me on the hunter pony day.'

'So?' Ellie frowned, not understanding. 'They probably just want to see you in the show. It's a big thing – the Royal International.'

'They haven't seen me since Christmas and now they want to turn up just cos there's something happening where they can play the proud parents.' He swore. 'Well, I don't want them there.'

Ellie couldn't imagine feeling like that about her parents. She'd have given anything to have them still alive and able to come and watch. But she knew Luke's childhood had been totally different from hers. His dad had often been away working, and his mum had travelled with him, so Luke was sent to boarding school at seven and spent most of his holidays at Len's house. Luke once told Ellie that Len had been more of a father to him than his dad ever was.

Luke folded his arms angrily. For a moment Ellie had the unfamiliar urge to comfort him. 'Hey, don't worry,' she said, her voice softening. 'There'll be so much to do at the show. I bet you can avoid them and I'll help you get away from them if you need.'

He managed a smile. 'Thanks.'

Just then there was the sound of a horsebox drawing into the car park. 'I bet that's the new horse. Let's go and see,' Ellie said.

They walked curiously to the car park. Len was there before them.

'Got here at last,' said the groom driving the lorry. He jumped out and handed Len some papers. As Len checked through them, the groom let down the ramp and winked at Ellie. 'This baby for you?'

'Oh no, I'm not Anna Hallett,' Ellie said quickly, biting back a smile at the thought. She watched as the groom brought a dark bay horse out. He walked quietly down the ramp. Ellie frowned. Usually, as soon as she saw a new horse, she had a feeling about it, sensing whether it was happy or stressed, anxious or laid-back, but with this one she felt nothing. She looked at the horse, reaching out with her mind, but all she found was a blank.

Whistling, the groom stripped off the horse's travelling boots, rug and tail guard. 'Where do you want him then?' he asked Len.

'I'll take him,' Ellie offered.

Len nodded.

'He's a stunner,' said Luke, walking round and taking in the horse's delicate head, his perfect conformation.

'Looks quiet too,' commented Len.

'Oh, Rocky's a lamb in the stable,' said the groom

quickly. 'We've had him six months. Never had a moment's problem with him.'

'And he's already been backed?' said Len.

'Yeah. Quiet as a donkey to ride. Right.' The groom handed the leadrope to Ellie. 'I'd best be off.'

Ellie clicked her tongue. She felt a moment's tension run through the horse, but then he turned and followed her, his head low. She looked at him curiously as she led him to his new stable. His eyes seemed strange. Usually, horses' eyes were so full of expression – they might be cheerful, wise, scared. Whatever a horse was feeling, she could always read something in its gaze. But this horse's eyes seemed completely dead of emotion. Unease prickled through her. She shut the door. The horse stood still, his head turned away from her. Something was definitely not right.

Ellie touched his neck and focused her mind, wondering what feelings she would pick up. She frowned. There was simply nothing there. She'd never felt anything like it. It was like a complete blank. She shut her eyes to concentrate harder.

You can talk to me if you want, she thought to the horse. *I can hear you.*

The air in the stable felt silent, blocked, like being underwater, and she had the sensation of fog swirling in her head . . .

'What are you doing?' Ellie jumped at the sound of Luke's voice. He had come to the door.

'Nothing,' she said, patting the horse's neck.

'Jeff sure knows how to pick them. First Lucifer. Now him,' Luke said admiringly.

Ellie nodded. But as she left the stable she took one last, long look at the horse, with the distinct feeling that something was really badly wrong.

I've never felt anything like it, she told Spirit as she stood with him that night. *I couldn't get any feelings from him. Nothing.*

Spirit sent her a picture of a stone wall.

For a moment she thought he was trying to say something about the field, but then she realized the meaning behind the picture. *Yes, that it! It's as if he's putting up a wall, that there's a barrier around him. I saw a fog too.*

Keep trying. She could feel Spirit's concern.

I will. Ellie had learnt enough to know that sometimes you just had to be patient and wait. You couldn't force a horse to talk to you. Sometimes all you could do was send it love and then it would eventually open its mind. It was just that she'd never felt such utter silence from a horse before.

At least I'm helping Lexi, she thought. After everyone had left the yard that night she had gone to the mare's stable and stood with her again, channelling healing energy, feeling the mare relax under her hands, her pain easing some more. Ellie suddenly remembered her other big news. *Oh, and Spirit – I'm buying Hope! My gran said I could!*

She felt his happiness.

I know I don't really need another horse, I've got you, but she's sweet and Uncle Len might have sold her otherwise. For some reason, Ellie felt the urge to make excuses.

It's good, Spirit reassured her. *I think you're meant to be together. I've always felt that.*

She's just a foal, Ellie said quickly. *It doesn't change anything between you and me.*

Spirit nuzzled her. *No, nothing will.*

Ellie felt a wave of happiness and rested her cheek against his. There was so much to look forward to, she realized – training Hope, the Royal International the following week, her birthday, and Luke's promise that they would celebrate it. What had he meant? Most of all, though, she felt happy because she had Spirit there to share everything with her just as he'd always done. She smiled. Yes. Life was good.

Chapter Six

Ellie had never been to a show like the Royal International before. As she rode down the hill late on Tuesday afternoon, she could see the vast Hickstead show ground sprawling out in front of her. There were stalls selling every kind of horsey paraphernalia, from breeches to horse food, and the main emerald-green arena looked very smart with its white stands and dazzling show jumps. The other arenas were dotted around the grounds.

Ellie stroked Picasso's glossy neck. It was amazing to be there. They had arrived the day before in two horseboxes. For the start of the show, Len had just brought the six hunter ponies and the two hunters who would be competing on Wednesday and Thursday. When the ponies had finished their classes on Wednesday, Helen would take them home and return with the remaining horses – the riding horses, hacks and intermediates.

Ellie had found it hard to get her head round all

the different types of classes when she'd first started living with her uncle, but now she knew that hunters were strong, handsome horses who could carry a person hunting all day; hacks were elegant and showy, bred to be the perfect horse for ladies and gentlemen to ride in the park; riding horses were not as showy as a hack but more refined than a hunter, and the intermediates were small hunters or riding horses ridden by riders aged twenty-five or under.

Len, Luke and Helen were all at the show with Ellie – Stuart and Sasha had stayed at home. As soon as they'd arrived on the show ground they had set up camp. Len and Luke were sleeping in the main lorry. Len's clients, the Armstrongs, owned the second lorry. Ellie and Helen were sharing a tent with a main section and two separate sleeping compartments. Ellie felt glad it was Helen at the show, not Sasha. Although she was getting on better with Sasha now, she still preferred Helen who was older and quieter. Helen was shy, kind and always gentle with the horses. She certainly wouldn't be up all night talking into her phone or partying wildly and Ellie was sure they'd get on just fine sharing a tent.

The horses were stabled in the show ground's temporary stables, which were on either side of the road leading up the hill to the horsebox park. It was noisy and dusty on the hill with the sounds of generators and music blaring out from people's caravans and horseboxes. There were queues for the toilets, the showers and the wash stations where horses could be bathed. The smell of burgers and hot dogs wafted around from the fast-food vans.

Ellie was struck by the difference between the dusty hill and the main show ground where everything was spotless and glamorous, the bowler-hatted and suited stewards walking around with clipboards and walkie-talkies, riders in their smart show clothes and visitors enjoying themselves shopping.

Picasso pulled at his bit, excited to be out, as she came through the security gate and rode alongside the large working-in area. It was really busy with people – she could see Luke there, exercising Hereward, one of the hunters. He had his reins in one hand, his dark grey T-shirt showing off his tanned arms and broad shoulders, his hair curling out from under his hat.

Two girls were walking along the path in shorts, boots and vest tops, their long hair carefully tousled. 'Who's that?' said one of them, indicating Luke.

'Luke Black,' replied the other.

The first girl looked hopeful. 'Do you know him?'

'Yeah.'

'Let's say hello then and see if he's going to the disco tonight.'

Ellie rolled her eyes as she watched the two girls hurry down to the ringside and call out to Luke. Ellie decided to ride somewhere else. Beyond the show rings there was a green hill where you could also ride, then a bridle path leading off across the fields. She headed over there and in the peace and quiet she schooled Picasso. Len had decided that Luke would ride Barney in the 15 hands-high working hunter pony class the next day so that Ellie could concentrate on Picasso, who was in the 14 hands-high class. Ellie didn't mind because she had Milly to ride too, and Fizz and Bill to prepare for the Armstrong children. After making sure Picasso was obedient and listening to her, she pushed him on up the hill, leaning forward and letting him really stretch out in a gallop.

He seemed to enjoy it, snorting and sidling around afterwards. Ellie grinned. 'That was fun, wasn't it, boy?' She did it once more and then set off over the fields to cool him down. It was very tranquil away from the show and all the people. Ellie brushed the flies away from Picasso's neck and thought about Spirit. She would miss him and Hope while she was at the show. Turning Picasso round, she wandered back with him in the afternoon sun towards the stables. She untacked him and washed him down, then returned to the lorry. Another show team was behind them – a caravan, tents and brightly coloured awnings set out alongside several gleaming horseboxes. A group of children and teenagers, aged from about seven to fourteen, chatted and generally messed around while some of their parents sat on chairs drinking wine and fruit juice. Ellie felt slightly wistful. They all seemed to be having such good fun. She'd been watching them since she'd arrived. Their trainer, Caroline, was as well known and successful as Len, but she had a very different approach, laughing with her team, joining in with their fun, chatting to the parents – while still insisting on one hundred per cent effort in the show ring. Ellie wished Len was like that, but, although he might talk to Luke, he rarely said anything that wasn't a command or a reprimand to her and Helen.

Ellie looked in her tent and in the living quarters of the lorry, but Helen wasn't there. Fetching an apple, she sat on the steps of the horsebox listening to the laughter and shrieks coming from the next-door team. Hearing the sound of footsteps, she looked up to see Luke returning after putting Hereward away.

'All on your own?'

She nodded.

'We can't have that. How about we get changed and go next door?'

Ellie hesitated. She was tired after the busy day and didn't know if she really felt like socializing with a whole load of new people.

'Come on, it'll be fun!' urged Luke.

'All right.' She gave in and went to the tent to get

changed. Once she'd put shorts and a T-shirt on, she brushed out the tangles in her blonde hair and went to the living quarters of the horsebox to wash her hands and face. She opened the door to see Luke in his boxer shorts.

'Sorry!' she gasped. She went to shut the door quickly.

'Don't be daft.' Luke stopped her. 'You *can* come in. I'm not butt-naked.'

Face burning, Ellie went to the sink. She didn't dare look up as she heard the sounds of Luke getting dressed. She didn't think she'd ever felt more embarrassed in her life! Even with her eyes looking firmly at the floor, she could still picture him standing there with almost no clothes on.

'It's OK, I'm respectable again,' Luke said at last. 'Well, as respectable as I'll ever be!' She glanced up and caught his grin. The living quarters suddenly seemed very small. She could feel the sink against her back. Her breath felt tight in her throat.

'Come on, let's go and have us some fun!' Pulling open the door, Luke leapt down the steps.

Taking a deep breath, Ellie followed him. *This is Luke*, she told herself strongly. *You don't like him in that way* at all, *remember!*

They went to the group of horseboxes and tents. Several of the grown-ups lifted their glasses and smiled in greeting.

'Hi, Luke,' said Caroline, the trainer.

'Hi, Caro. This is Ellie,' said Luke. 'Is it all right if we join in for a bit?'

'Sure.' Caroline smiled at Ellie. 'Help yourself to a drink. There's loads in the cool box.'

'You can come in here, Luke,' said an older girl with glossy blonde hair, looking out of one of the caravans.

'Come on,' Luke said to Ellie. He helped himself to a beer and she took a Coke, then they went into the caravan. Inside, there were three girls and two boys with several boxes of pizza on the table. Ellie recognized them all from the show ring, although they were older than she was so she didn't usually ride against them. A stick-thin red-haired boy who looked about eighteen was sitting on the table, while the blonde girl who'd invited them in was sorting out music on an iPod and speakers.

'Hi, guys,' Luke said. 'This is Ellie. Ellie this is Bea,' he said, nodding to the blonde girl. 'She's a friend of Anna's. And this is Liam.'

'Good to meet you,' said the red-haired boy. He had an Irish accent and a wide grin. Bea went over and put an arm round his neck and kissed him.

'Cut it out, you two!' groaned the stocky boy with sandy hair sitting on the sofa. He threw a beer mat at them. 'I'm Daniel,' he said to Ellie. 'This is my sister, Sam.' He nodded to the pretty dark-haired girl beside him who looked a bit younger than the others, about sixteen, and who was reading a magazine. Ellie recognized her from the working hunter pony and show hunter pony classes. Sam smiled at her. 'And this is Claire,' Daniel went on. Claire had a mass of brown curls and teasing eyes. She was cuddling a pink toy pig.

'You have to say hello to Egbert too,' she told Ellie. 'He's our mascot.' She waggled him in the air.

'Hi, Egbert,' said Ellie with a grin.

'Sit down,' said Sam, moving up on the bench so Ellie could squeeze on too. Luke helped himself to a slice of pizza, then pulled down a stool that folded into the breakfast bar and sat on that.

'So how are you doing?' Liam asked Luke. 'You're still with Anna then?'

'Yeah.' Luke grinned lazily.

'You'd better not two-time her, Luke,' Bea told him, flicking back her long blonde hair.

Luke gave her an innocent look. 'Would I?'

Liam chuckled.

'You can two-time her with me any time, Luke!' Claire laughed raucously.

'Oh, Claire, you are *way* out of my league!' Luke grinned and took a magazine from the table. 'Where are the horoscopes?' he said, flicking through. 'Here we go. What does tomorrow hold?' He stabbed his finger at the paper. 'Sagittarius, that's me: "you're on a winning streak".' He nodded. 'I like that. Championship, here I come. And love rating: five out of five stars.'

'It's always that for you,' commented Daniel.

Luke cocked an eyebrow at Ellie. 'Leo for you. "Face each challenge as it comes and you will win through." And love beckons, Ellie!'

Claire nudged her. 'Sounds all right to me!'

Ellie blushed.

Claire took the paper. 'Woo-hoo,' she said. 'Listen to this – "it may seem a mountain, but you can succeed and hot love awaits." So that's me and Duke winning the 15-handers and then at the disco, well . . .' She ran her finger teasingly down Daniel's back. '*Hot love!*'

'Gerroff!' Daniel pulled a face and wriggled away. 'Sorry, I always have this effect on girls,' he sighed to Ellie.

'And pigs!' Claire said, stuffing Egbert down his back.

The joking and messing around went on. Ellie didn't say much. Her thoughts were full of the next day and she was starting to really miss Spirit. She wished she could go and talk to him as she usually did. She wondered if he was missing her and that thought took all the party feeling out of her, and left her waiting for a point when she could return to her tent without seeming rude. At last everyone decided to go to the disco that was held every night in a big marquee in the middle of the horsebox park.

'If it's no good we'll come and party back here,' said Bea. 'Tomorrow we really must have a good time when the hunter pony classes are over. Anna's arriving then, isn't she, Luke?'

Luke nodded. 'And my olds. They're coming to watch for once.' He sounded unbothered, but Ellie knew him well enough to hear the slight tightness that crept into his voice at the mention of his parents.

She glanced over at him, but he was already jumping to his feet. 'What are we sitting round here for? Let's hit that disco!'

Ellie made her excuses, saying she wanted an early night, and left them to it. Pulling on a hoody to ward off the chill evening air, she went to the stables. All her uncle's horses and ponies were next to each other. It was peaceful in their stalls. She went into all of them, straightening their rugs, stroking them, saying goodnight. First to the two hunters – Hereward and Oscar – then moving on to the ponies: Picasso, Milly, Wisp, Barney, Fizz and Bill. Wisp and Picasso were looking anxious and were pacing around, so Ellie did her best to soothe them. She thought wistfully about Spirit. When he'd been alive, he had often travelled to the shows with the team. The more nervous horses had always responded well to his calmness.

She moved on to Barney who was cheerfully eating his hay. He snorted and wiped his nose on her T-shirt.

'Thanks, boy,' she told him, but she gave him a hug. The people who'd been to see him had decided to buy him. The Royal International would be his last show for her uncle's team before he went to his new home, but at least she'd liked the family. The girl was twelve and wouldn't grow out of him for a long time. She was a great rider too and had fed him plenty of Polos in the stable. Ellie was sure Barney would have a good home with her. 'Be good tomorrow,' she told him. He looked at her, his eyes cheeky.

Ellie left the stables and went back to her tent. Her uncle was at the pub. Helen had gone round to a friend's lorry and Luke was still out at the disco with the others. All around, she could hear the sound of the generators and music. Ellie changed into her nightclothes and climbed into her sleeping bag. She had a book with her and read it by torchlight until she started falling asleep. Then she settled down for the night. Tomorrow would be her big day in the show ring.

Oh, Spirit, she thought. *I really wish you were here.*

Hugging her arms around herself, she curled up, pulling the sleeping bag tightly over her and fell asleep.

Chapter Seven

Ellie's alarm went off at 4 a.m. She and Helen dragged themselves out of bed in the dark to help prepare Wisp and Milly for the early classes. But when they reached the stables they found Len and Luke were already there. Len's face looked like thunder. He marched past Ellie, almost knocking her over.

'What's going on?' Ellie asked Luke.

Luke ran a hand through his hair. 'It's Wisp. He cut his ear in the night. It's not bad, but it will need a few stitches.'

'Oh no.' Ellie's face fell. Wisp couldn't go in his class with a stitched ear.

'Great start!' Luke said.

Helen and Ellie went to see Wisp. The pony seemed unbothered by the wound on his ear, but it would definitely rule him out of the ring. 'I'll clean him up,' said Helen, patting him. 'You get Milly ready.'

Ellie went into Milly's stall. The chestnut pony whickered and came over, searching for treats. Ellie fed her a Polo and then plaited her up. She would work her in, then wash her off and groom her properly. Their class was due to start at 9 a.m.

Without Wisp to get ready, the team had more time on their hands. While Ellie prepared Milly, Helen and Luke saw to the other ponies. They all worked hard, exercising, grooming, plaiting, each knowing what needed to be done.

At just before nine o'clock, Ellie was sitting on Milly by the entrance to the ring with the other ponies who were in her class. Luke did the final preparations, wiping over the tack, adding more fly repellant, oiling Milly's hooves. Her coat shone like a conker fresh out of its shell; her flaxen mane was rolled into neat plaits. Ellie could feel the butterflies in her stomach as she caught sight of her uncle watching from the side of the ring.

The steward undid the rope stretched across the ring entrance. 'Class 136!' he called.

'Good luck!' Luke told Ellie as she took a breath. 'Remember you'll be doing the gallop up the hill. It's a long way, don't start too early or she'll run out of steam by the time she passes the judges. Equally, don't let her just take off and get out of control.'

'OK,' Ellie said, taking it all in.

'You can do it!' he told her.

'Thanks!'

Buoyed up by the confidence in his eyes, she rode

Milly into the ring. The short grass felt springy under the pony's neat hooves. Milly walked out. The stands at the side of the ring were filling up with spectators. It was a perfect day. The ring was large with trees inside it, their dark green leaves casting shadows on the grass. Ellie kept a careful eye on the two judges and stewards. More and more ponies filed in. Ellie saw Sam from the night before. She was riding a striking dun pony. All the ponies there that day had won a class earlier in the year to qualify, so the standard was very high.

'Be good,' Ellie breathed to Milly as the pony moved her head up and down. She glanced to the centre, hoping the judge hadn't seen, and cursed inside as she saw both judges watching her. The steward called to them all to trot on.

As always, the ponies walked, trotted and cantered round the ring together and then galloped up the long side. There were so many ponies, the round seemed to go on forever. Ellie thought Milly had done well apart from a nasty moment where she had almost switched legs in the canter, which would have been a very bad mistake to make and one she would certainly have lost marks for.

The steward brought them all back to a walk and then pulled them into a line in a provisional order. Milly was lying fourth. Ellie patted her. Hopefully, they could make up any lost ground in the individual show. She waited her turn, then rode out to the judge and bowed.

As she started her show, she could feel the pony bristling with the joy of being in the ring. Ellie knew she'd have her hands full getting through the show without Milly deciding to pull or canter on the wrong leg. Concentrating hard, she just about managed to contain Milly's liveliness, although in the gallop Milly's exuberance took hold and she set off very quickly. Ellie managed to control her, but only just. She gave a big smile to the judges as she bowed at the end and then rode back to the line, feeling shaky with relief that it was over and she'd done OK.

Len came into the ring to help her remove the saddle. 'Good riding,' he said guardedly.

Ellie took a breath and held Milly as he pulled the saddle off and gave the pony a brush over. There was just the conformation section next and then the judges would make their decision . . .

When all the ponies had been walked and trotted in hand, the two judges got together. Ellie was back on Milly now and her uncle had left the ring. She could see Luke watching from the ringside.

How had she done? The first two ponies had both done really good shows, the third-placed one had become over excited and hadn't slowed down well after his gallop. The places were called in reverse order, starting with eighth place. A commentator came into the ring and called the numbers into a microphone. Every time a number was called, the pony was ridden out to take a place in the winning line-up and there were cheers from the supporters in the stand.

Eighth place was called, seventh, sixth, fifth . . .

Ellie could feel her hands starting to sweat in her gloves. Another pony was called in for fourth place. Would she be out of the ribbons completely?

'Number 132,' said the steward, pointing at Ellie. Third place! It wasn't a win, but it was still brilliant to be placed so high at such an important show.

Patting Milly hard, Ellie rode out to loud applause and then listened as the final two ponies were also called out. Sam won the class on the dun pony. There was a massive cheer in the stands from Caroline's team. Then one of the judges walked along the line, presenting the rosettes from a basket. Ellie tied hers to the string on her number, tucked the tails into her jacket pocket and then followed the winners round for a lap of honour. It was amazing to be cantering round such a big ring with so many people clapping. Ellie followed the second-placed pony out of the ring as Sam went on for the final lap on her own.

Luke and Len met Ellie.

'Not bad, lass,' said Len, before striding away to do a final check for Oliver Armstrong who was riding Bill in the next class.

Ellie jumped off Milly and hugged her. 'Congratulations!' she called to Sam as she rode past.

'Thanks!' Sam beamed.

'You did really well,' Luke said to Ellie.

'Mmm. It wasn't a win, though,' said Ellie. Their eyes met and she knew he understood how she felt. She was pleased with the yellow rosette, but she also knew that on another day Milly might have won that class. Still, that was showing. Sometimes you could do the best performance you'd ever done and the judge simply might not like your pony. At least that hadn't happened. Ellie knew in her heart that the two ponies placed ahead of her had performed better and deserved to be higher placed that day.

'You still have Picasso to go,' Luke said. 'There's the chance of a win yet.'

'Yeah, and you have Barney to ride,' she reminded him.

'I'd better fetch him,' said Luke, but just then a man's voice called his name.

Ellie saw Luke jump and glance round. A tall, good-looking man in his fifties, with greying hair, was coming towards them. His eyes were the same bright blue as Luke's, but instead of being teasing, they were hard.

'Oh, great,' Luke muttered. He squared his shoulders as the man reached them. 'Hi. Richard, this is Ellie. Ellie, this is my father – Richard.'

Not 'Dad', Ellie noticed.

'Nice to meet you,' she said politely to the older man. She could feel the tension coming from Luke. She remembered everything he'd told her about his father, how he had never been there for him when he was younger, how he had rarely done anything with him, always being too busy working or doing other things.

Now the introductions were made, neither Luke nor his dad seemed to know what to say. Richard stuffed his hands in his pockets.

'Where's Angela?' Luke asked briefly.

'Your mother's still at the hotel. You know she doesn't like getting up early. She'll be here to see you ride later, though. Twelve thirty, Len said.'

Luke nodded.

'So how was your first class?' his father asked.

'I couldn't go in.'

'Wisp injured himself,' Ellie added.

Luke's father didn't even bother to ask if the pony was OK. 'You've got a decent chance of winning your next class, though, haven't you?' he said to Luke, who shrugged.

'Maybe.'

'We should go,' Ellie put in hastily, feeling the tension growing in Luke by the second. 'We need to sort the horses out. We'll see you later, Mr Black.'

'Yes. I'll be at the ringside for your class,' Richard said to Luke.

Luke gave the smallest of nods.

'Come on,' said Ellie, remembering her promise to help him escape from his parents when he needed to. Luke didn't say anything as they led Milly back towards the hill. Ellie stole a glance at him. His expression was brooding.

'So,' she said. 'Want to talk about it?'

'Nope.'

'He didn't seem that bad,' she volunteered.

Luke swung round, bitterness clear in his eyes. 'Oh no, he's not that bad. Not unless you're a six-year-old boy who loves your dad so much you beg him to come out with you or let you go with him, but then you're constantly told no, he's too busy. Just as he was always too busy when I was seven, eight, nine and ten, as well. And then I just became a bother to him when I didn't get along at school and his time was "wasted" by my head teachers calling him in.'

Luke glared. 'He pushed me to one side all the time I was growing up, Ellie. How do you think that felt? He never wanted to spend time with me. Weekends he was working. Holidays he was travelling and I was sent to Len's. He had no time for me then. I don't want him in my life now!'

He strode on ahead of her. Ellie pulled Milly into a trot and caught up with him. She felt the hurt radiating from him in strong, hot waves. She touched his shoulder, knowing there was nothing she could say to make things better. Just as for horses, sometimes all she could do was be there to hear them. She couldn't change the bad things that had happened, but she could help by understanding.

'It's awful,' she said softly. 'I agree. I'm sorry it was like that. It shouldn't have been.'

Their eyes met and for a moment it was as though she was seeing deep down inside him, all his usual barriers down. He let out a deep breath. 'I don't normally talk about this stuff.'

She shrugged, knowing he wouldn't want her to make a big deal out of it. 'You've listened to me enough in the past. It's OK.'

He put an arm round her shoulders and gave her a quick, warm hug. 'Thanks. Though I don't want to talk about it any more. But thanks for listening and not saying anything stupid.' He smiled, looking more like his usual self. 'Tomorrow I shall repay you by celebrating your birthday in style.'

'What? At the disco?' Ellie teased.

'I might even treat you to a burger if you're lucky – with cheese!'

She rolled her eyes. 'Wow, I can barely wait!'

They grinned and walked together up the hill to the stables.

Chapter Eight

Luke's teasing mood didn't last for long. When he arrived on Barney for the start of his class, both his parents were standing at the ringside with Len, his mum in a black-and-white zebra-print dress. She was very slim and glamorous, with long, glossy brown hair and smooth skin.

'She looks really young,' Ellie said to Luke as he brought Barney over to where she was standing.

Luke raised his eyebrows. 'It's amazing what Botox, the odd nip-and-tuck and hours at the gym can do. I hope she doesn't scare the horses in that dress.'

Ellie glanced at him. 'You OK?'

'Sure! Why wouldn't I be?' But as Luke rode away she saw him give Barney an uncharacteristically sharp leg aid. The pony jogged. 'Walk!' Luke snapped.

Barney, used to Joe and Ellie's gentle riding, protested by swishing his tail and tucking his nose in mutinously. Ellie chewed her lip. Barney wasn't the most sensitive pony, but he didn't like to be pushed around. Luke rode him into a figure of eight, keeping his reins short and his legs on. Barney deliberately seemed to go on the wrong leg in protest. Luke, who was usually supremely laid-back and relaxed when he was riding, now looked tense.

'Luke!' Ellie went after him. 'Calm down. Don't get wound up just because your parents are here.'

'I'm not wound up!' he said sharply as he rode on past.

Ellie sighed and went over to where Luke's parents were talking to Len. 'Can I have the grooming kit? I'll give Barney a brush before he goes in.'

'You must be Ellie,' Luke's mum said as Len handed the basket over. 'I'm Angela.'

'Hi.' Close up, Ellie could see that everything about Luke's mum was immaculate – her nails were painted a bright, flawless red and her make-up was perfect. She looked as if she had never been messy in her life.

'So we're expecting good things in this class?' Luke's father said to Len.

'Aye. The pony's a cracker – he's won almost every time out this year. It's a difficult course, no two ways about it, but he should jump it no problem. Luke's a good rider.' A rare smile crossed Len's face. 'Reminds me of when I was a lad.'

'You've been very good to him,' Angela said lightly.

'We do appreciate it, Len. I don't know what we'd have done if you hadn't let him come and stay with you. He's always loved it at your house. It's been like a second home to him.'

First home. Ellie bit back the sharp words just in time.

Richard turned to Len. 'He just didn't have the right temperament for boarding school.'

'He was such a difficult child,' sighed Angela. 'He really needed somewhere like your yard, Len.'

No, he needed parents who were there for him and loved him, Ellie thought angrily. She could see exactly why Luke felt so bitter towards his parents; they talked about him as if he was a dog or a horse. She felt a rush of protective sympathy. No wonder he was wary of loving anything or anyone apart from Pip.

Barney was jogging and pulling now. Ellie decided not to say anything but just help clean him up and get him ready.

'Good luck!' she called when Luke finally rode into the ring.

Luke was very tense. From the moment he pushed Barney into a canter and the pony took off on the wrong leg, Ellie had a bad feeling about the round. The fences were large and imposing, all made from rustic poles and hedges rather than the brightly coloured jumps in the show-jumping classes. Usually

Barney jumped beautifully, but feeling the tension in Luke, he played up, rushing at the fences and fighting for his head. Ellie groaned as he knocked fences seven and eight down, and when Luke smacked him, he ground to a halt at jump number nine.

Ellie glanced over at her uncle. He had a face like thunder. Luke's parents were looking disappointed.

'Just get round the rest safely,' Ellie prayed.

Barney didn't knock anything else down, but Luke rode through the finish grim-faced. He had to ride into the second ring immediately, where the second judge was waiting to watch his individual show. Barney went on the wrong leg on his second canter strike-off. It was clear his chance in the class was completely over.

Len strode over to help Luke unsaddle Barney for the conformation section. He looked furious. 'You blew it!' he hissed. 'You completely messed up.'

'I know – all right!' Luke muttered.

'You could have won that class. What happened in there?'

'It was just one of those things!' The steward motioned to Luke to go in and he made his escape by leading Barney into the ring.

'Sodding idiot!' snapped Len, marching away.

Luke led Barney out of the ring after the show. Ellie helped him tack up in silence. His parents came over.

'Well, that wasn't the greatest performance,' his father commented.

Luke didn't say anything.

'You should have ridden him forward, got him moving more.'

'Do *not* give me riding advice!' Luke ground out.

'Now, Luke. Your father's only trying to be helpful,' his mother chided.

'Well, I don't need his help!' Furious, Luke led Barney away.

'See? What can you do?' his mum said to his dad, spreading her hands.

Ellie ran after Luke, but he was vaulting on Barney. Without looking back, he trotted down the path and up towards the stables. Ellie raced after him. She was out of breath by the time she reached the horsebox. Luke had untacked Barney and was letting him graze, talking and laughing with Bea, Liam and Daniel from next door.

'Are . . . are you OK?' Ellie panted.

'Of course I am.' Luke shrugged as if nothing had happened. 'Why?'

She stared at him. 'Your parents –'

'What about them?' he cut in. 'I'm fine, Ellie.'

'Well, apart from just having got a load of faults in the ring!' put in Liam.

'Yeah, well,' Luke said flippantly, 'I have to give the rest of you a chance some of the time.'

'Very generous of you,' said Bea dryly.

'You look hot,' said Liam to Ellie.

'I could cool you down with the hose?' offered Daniel.

'No, thanks,' Ellie said hastily.

'Oh, go on. I could spray all of the girls. We could have a wet T-shirt competition,' teased Daniel.

'A wet T-shirt competition?' purred a voice from behind them. 'Now *that* sounds interesting. But only if it's the boys.'

Ellie's heart sank. *Anna Hallett.* The dark-haired girl walked up to them. She was wearing denim hot pants with brown boots that showed off her long, tanned legs.

'Hey, gorgeous,' she greeted Luke, walking over to kiss him on the lips. 'Glad to see me?'

'You bet, babe,' he said, kissing her back lingeringly.

Ellie looked away sharply.

'How did your class go then?' Anna said when they finally broke apart.

'Not so great.' Luke shrugged. 'But who cares? Should we go and find a drink?'

'Sounds good to me,' said Anna.

'We'll come along,' chimed in Liam and Bea.

'Here, Ellie. Take Barney.' Luke threw Barney's leadrope at her.

'But, Luke, there's loads to do!' Ellie protested. 'Don't just go off!'

'See ya!' he called, setting off down the hill with his arm round Anna's shoulders.

Ellie could have stamped her foot in frustration. She hated the act Luke was putting on and there was so much to do with the horses. Barney needed washing down, but she also had to get Picasso out; his class was next. Fizz also needed preparing for the hunter pony lead-rein class that afternoon, and Bill had come second in his class in the morning with Oliver, which meant he was due in the main ring for the overall hunter pony championship at 3 p.m. *Thanks for nothing, Luke*, she thought as she quickly led Barney to the wash station.

To Ellie's relief, Helen arrived back at the lorry and took over with Barney while Ellie tacked up Picasso.

'What about walking the course? Do you know where Luke is?' Helen asked. 'You'll need him to hold Picasso for you while you walk the course.'

'I'll try ringing him,' said Ellie. But Luke's phone was switched off.

'Don't worry. Stay calm,' instructed Helen. 'I'll come with you and then dash back here to get Fizz and Bill ready.'

'But it's such a long way from here to the ring!' protested Ellie.

'I know, but you can't go there on your own. If Len's at the ringside, I'll come straight back.'

But Len had expected Luke to be helping Ellie and he was nowhere to be seen. Helen held Picasso while Ellie walked round the course, checking the jumps, assessing the angles of the fences and counting strides between the combinations so that she could give Picasso the best ride possible. She found out from Sam, who was walking the course too, that there hadn't been many clears in Luke's class in the end. It was a tricky course, but Ellie was sure Picasso would cope with it.

'Thanks,' she said gratefully to Helen when she returned to Picasso. 'I should be all right now. Len will turn up for the class – Luke's bound to, as well.'

'OK, see you later!' said Helen, breaking into a run.

'I'll come and help as soon as I've finished!' Ellie called after her, feeling bad that Helen had to prepare Fizz and Bill on her own.

She started riding Picasso round again. Just before the class started Len appeared. 'Where's Luke?' he asked.

Ellie shrugged. She might be fed up with Luke, but she wouldn't cause trouble for him.

Her uncle shook his head and started to run a cloth expertly over Picasso's coat. 'I don't know what the hell's going on with him today, but he'd flamin' well better snap out of it.'

Ellie stared. Her uncle knew Luke better than most

people – he'd given him a home for most of his life, treated him like a son. Could he really not work out why Luke might not be his usual self that day?

'To mess things up – at a show like this . . .'

'Maybe it had something to do with the fact his parents are here?' Ellie said, unable to stop herself. 'I mean, maybe that could have upset him?'

Her uncle frowned. 'It better bloody not be that. What does it matter who's watching you? You get in the ring and you do your stuff. End of story.'

His eyes were stony. Feeling Ellie tighten the reins angrily, Picasso fidgeted. With a supreme effort, she forced herself to control her temper. She wasn't going to do anyone any favours by getting mad. It wouldn't help Luke and she could just imagine her uncle's mood if *she* messed up in the ring too.

The steward opened the rope across the entrance and called her number.

Ellie clicked her tongue and rode forward. She wished Luke had come to watch her, but as she rode through the entrance she pushed all thoughts away and concentrated on Picasso and the jumping course ahead. The dark bay pony had so much energy and power – at just the touch of her heels he could move up a gear into a gallop and he had a massive jump. The challenge was keeping him sweet; not letting him put a buck in after a fence, encouraging him to show off without going over the top. Ellie had put hours of training into him, being shouted at by her uncle, falling off, riding him on her own, and she had ridden him in for ages earlier that day. It all paid off. With the sun shining down, she jumped the best round of her life. Picasso cleared every fence without hesitation, his hooves tucked up neatly, his ears pricked. As they flew through the finish at a gallop, they heard a massive round of applause from the spectators in the stand. Ellie was overjoyed and patted him again and again. Picasso loved the clapping and praise and nodded his head up and down, as if inviting more.

There was barely time to catch her breath before she was in the conformation ring. Still on a high from the jumping, they both performed a foot-perfect show. The conformation ring was small and slightly cramped, but they managed a gallop at the end before she pulled him up and halted in front of the judges, beaming. They smiled back and Ellie felt a rush of triumph. She'd done everything she possibly could.

Her uncle thought so too. As she took Picasso out of the ring to strip his tack off and complete the final phase of the class, he strode over, his face delighted. 'You nailed it, lass!' he exclaimed. 'Excellent work.'

Ellie could have dropped through the ground in surprise. It was the most praise her uncle had ever given her. 'Picasso was brilliant,' she said, stroking the pony, who accepted her pats with a slightly haughty expression.

'You rode him flamin' well. Luke could take a lesson or two from your book.'

Luke. Ellie's happiness sank a notch or two as she realized he hadn't been there to see her round. She couldn't help feeling hurt. They usually always stood at the ringside, cheering each other on. She'd been there for him, but just because he was upset about his parents being there he'd walked off and forgotten about her.

Trying not to think about it, she led Picasso into the ring and walked and trotted him out for the judge.

At last she was done, Picasso had been marked and all she could do was wait until the end of the class to hear the judges' decision. As she waited, Luke's parents came over. 'Do you know where Luke is?' his father asked.

Ellie shook her head. 'Sorry.'

'We really wanted to see him. We thought we'd have a chance to spend time with him after his class,' Angela said, looking put out. 'We came all this way.'

Ellie hesitated. 'I can text him for you.' She took out her phone and turned it on. No messages from Luke. Not even a good luck. She tried phoning him, but he didn't answer so she texted him instead: *Yr mum and dad are here by the ring. They want to c u. Can u come? Ex*

A moment later a text flashed up. She clicked on VIEW.

2 busy enjoying myself. L.

That was it. No asking her how she'd done. Nothing. Just that he was 'too busy enjoying himself'. Anger swept through her.

'From Luke?' his mum said, and Ellie realized they'd seen her reading the new text.

'Yeah. I'm sorry, but he says he's too busy.' She didn't want to but she lied for him. 'There're just so many ponies to get ready today.' *And Anna to hang around with* . . . she added in her head, thinking of poor Helen being rushed off her feet back at the lorry.

Luke's mother looked irritated. 'I knew he'd be like this,' she said to Luke's dad. 'I don't know why we bothered coming. He's so selfish!'

Ellie only just stopped her mouth from falling open. OK, Luke was selfish and behaving badly that day, but couldn't his mother see *why* he acted as he did? She put her foot in the stirrup. 'I'd better keep Picasso moving,' she said, riding away.

When the class results were announced over the loudspeaker, Ellie stood with her uncle, wishing Luke was there as the numbers were read out. Sixth place, fifth, fourth, third, second . . .

Ellie crossed her fingers, her stomach filled with butterflies. *Please, please, please*, she prayed.

'And in first place, number 272, Ellie Carrington riding Woodhouse Picasso!'

'You did it, lass!' exclaimed Len.

Ellie felt elation explode through her. People nearby started to congratulate her. The steward ushered Picasso in and she trotted him to the top of the line, where she was presented with a blue rosette – the first place rosettes at the Royal International were always blue, unlike those of most shows, and a blue sash was placed around Picasso's neck.

'A beautiful round! Well done!' the judge smiled, patting Picasso. 'He's a fantastic pony.'

Ellie had to stand for pictures and then set off on the lap of honour. It was brilliant to be leading it and when she rode round for the second time on her own she let him thunder down the long side, her grin stretching from ear to ear as the crowd clapped.

'We did it!' she whispered to Picasso as she leant forward against his neck. 'We won!' It was the best feeling ever!

Ellie came down to earth with a bump when she finally returned to the horsebox. Helen had been texting Luke too, but he had ignored her and she'd been trying to get everything ready on her own. Ellie joined in, but now there was the added task of preparing Picasso for the overall working hunter pony championship, which would take place after the 13 hands-high class and was open to the first and second place winners in each of the three working hunter pony classes.

There was so much to do. As usual, the Armstrong children did nothing to help. They couldn't even be bothered to walk up the hill to the stables, but simply waited at the ring for Ellie and Helen to bring their ponies to them.

However, despite the rush, it was a successful afternoon, with Emmie Armstrong coming fourth in the lead-rein class and Oliver Armstrong scooping the Reserve Supreme Champion in the show-hunter pony championship in the main ring. Ellie went one better when Picasso won his championship and became working hunter pony Supreme Champion. She saw Luke in the stands, laughing with Anna, Bea, Liam, Daniel and Claire. They all cheered as she won and Luke gave her a thumbs-up. She rode out of the ring, expecting him to come over and congratulate her, but he had already gone off again.

Ellie could feel anger and hurt simmering inside. She and Helen had done everything they could to prevent Len realizing Luke wasn't around helping. Luckily, Len had been with the Armstrongs and Ellie was sure her uncle thought Luke was working with her.

But he's not, she thought to herself as she wearily rugged Picasso up and then checked the other horses' haynets and water. They were all in their stalls now – the day's work finally done. *He's off having a good time.*

She went back to the lorry and found Helen sitting on the ramp, looking completely exhausted. Her face was pale and she had her head in her hands.

'Hey,' Ellie looked at her in concern. 'You OK?'

'I've got such a headache,' Helen groaned. 'And there's still the tack to clean and the lorry to sort.'

'I'm not surprised you've got a headache. You've been working like a mad thing all day. Have you eaten?'

Helen shook her head. 'Not since breakfast.'

'But that's nuts.' Even Ellie had found time to grab a hot dog mid-morning. 'You've been up since 4 a.m. Stay there. I'll bring you something, then we can do the tack together.'

Ellie hurried past the horseboxes to the nearest burger van and bought cups of tea and burgers for Helen and herself. She carried them back carefully on a cardboard tray. When she returned, she found Helen holding a pair of Luke's show breeches in her hands and staring at them.

'What are you doing with those?' Ellie said.

Helen looked up. 'Luke's just given them to me.' There was a note of disbelief in her voice. 'He said he wants me to wash them for him for tomorrow.'

Ellie stared at her. 'You've got to be joking!'

Helen gave a slightly hysterical laugh. 'Nope. He just came by with Anna and those friends of his from next door, gave me his breeches and said could I wash them for tomorrow.'

Ellie was already shaking her head. 'Oh, that is *it*! He's not getting away with this. Not after skiving off this afternoon!' Her temper exploded and she put the tray down hard, spilling the tea. 'I've had enough.' She grabbed the breeches and marched round the ramp.

Chapter Nine

'Ellie, where are you going?' Helen called.

Ellie ignored her. She had never felt so cross. How dare Luke just give Helen his breeches! How dare he not help and get things ready for the next day!

She could hear music and laughter coming from Bea's caravan. She stormed in. Luke was lounging on the sofa, his arm round Anna. Bea and Liam were next to them. They were all laughing at Daniel and Claire who were doing an imitation of *Strictly Come Dancing*.

'Hey,' Luke said, seeing Ellie. 'Come to join us?'

'No, I haven't!' she snapped. 'I've come to give you these!'

She held up his breeches.

'Oooh, now where did you get those, Ellie?' Claire said suggestively.

Daniel laughed. 'Yeah, did you know about this, Anna?'

Anna giggled. 'Maybe there's something you're not telling me, Luke.'

The way she spoke showed she clearly didn't think of Ellie as the slightest threat, which sent Ellie's fury even more sky high. 'You've done nothing this afternoon, Luke!' she blazed. 'You haven't lifted a finger to help. You didn't even come to see me in the ring!' For a moment she saw a flash of contrition in his eyes, but she was too mad to stop. 'Stop being so selfish! Helen's exhausted. There's tack to clean, the lorry to tidy and all you're doing is sitting in here. If you want your breeches washed, then do them yourself!'

Opening the bin, she threw the breeches inside along with the dirty takeaway boxes and teabags.

'Ellie! What the hell are you doing?' Luke leapt to his feet, the contrition vanishing from his face. 'They'll stain!'

Ellie swung round and marched out.

Daniel whooped and clapped. She could hear Liam, Bea and Claire laughing.

'She's gone nuts!' Anna gasped.

Luke flung open the door of the caravan. 'Ellie!' he yelled furiously.

She marched round the side of the lorry, rage pounding in her ears. Stopping on the far side, she took a breath.

Helen was there. 'What was that about? What did you do?' she gasped.

Ellie could feel her anger starting to subside. 'Gave Luke his breeches back.' She felt a grin tug at her mouth. 'I don't think he'll be asking you to wash them again.'

'Why?' Helen looked much better now she'd had some food and a drink.

Ellie grinned. 'Come on. I'll tell you while we sort the lorry.'

Ellie went to bed early that night. She knew it was going to be another 4 a.m. start the next morning, with Oscar going in the first hunter class at 7.30 a.m.

No lie-in for me on my birthday, she thought ruefully as she climbed into her sleeping bag.

Helen had already gone to bed too. Len was out at the pub again and she had no idea where Luke was – probably at the disco with Anna. As Ellie thought about him, she felt angry all over again. She hated him when he was as selfish as he'd been that day. Yes, sure, he'd been upset about seeing his parents, but it was no excuse to treat everyone else badly. *Stupid idiot*, she thought. For a moment she remembered stuffing his breeches in the bin. Had he washed them and removed the stains? What did it matter?

Turning over on her side, she pushed all thoughts of Luke firmly out of her mind and went to sleep.

'*Happy birthday to you! Happy birthday to you!*'

Ellie woke to the sound of Luke's singing. Her alarm hadn't gone off yet. She sat up, disorientated, blinking like a mole. Where was she? Seeing the canvas all around her, she remembered she was in the tent.

'*Happy birthday, dear Ellie . . .*' The door to her sleeping compartment opened and Luke poked his head in. '*Happy birthday to you!*'

Grinning, he thrust a bacon sandwich into her hands.

'Luke! What are you doing?' She glanced at her alarm clock and saw it was 7 a.m. Her heart almost jumped out of her chest. 'I've overslept!' She started to scramble out of her sleeping bag.

'Don't worry,' Luke said. 'I changed your alarm clock to give you a lie-in.'

'You did what?' She stared at him, dumbfounded.

'It's your birthday. I told Helen to have a lie-in too and I got Hereward and Oscar ready. We're only putting the two of them in the ring today. It was no big deal.' Ellie sat back, her brain trying to readjust. Something he'd just said came back to her. 'You came in here and changed my alarm clock?'

'Yep!' he said, grinning. 'You look cute asleep, you know. Like Sleeping Beauty with your hair spread all around.'

Ellie blushed. The thought of Luke coming in and seeing her while she was asleep was very unsettling.

'Here you are! It's not a birthday without presents,' Luke said, putting a package on her sleeping bag. 'I wondered about giving you flowers or chocolates, but I thought you might like these better.'

Ellie looked inside. She saw a bag of horse treats, a new pair of show gloves and a small purple box. She opened the box. Inside, there was a silver chain with a tiny pendant of a show horse trotting.

'Luke!' She felt lost for words. She looked up into his blue eyes. 'It's beautiful.'

'It's just something small. I'm sorry about yesterday,' he said ruefully. 'I was an idiot. It was just, well, you know . . .'

As his words trailed off, she felt the last of her anger vanish. She couldn't stay cross with him.

'I'll make up for it today. You and Helen can have an easy day and I'll do all the work, then tonight I'll take you out and we can celebrate your birthday. Deal?'

She swallowed, still touched by the gifts and the fact he'd been thoughtful enough to give her and Helen a lie-in. 'Deal.'

'Happy birthday,' he said again, leaning forward to kiss her forehead. She pulled her head back in surprise and his lips missed her forehead, brushing instead against her mouth. Ellie felt a sharp jolt run through her. She stared at him, eyes wide.

'Well, that was unexpected,' he said, looking at her softly. 'But unexpectedly nice.' She found she couldn't look away from him. He smiled as he moved back.

'You'd better get up now, though, or Len will be on the war path – and that bacon sandwich will go cold.'

She nodded, and then to her relief he was gone, the flap falling back across her sleeping compartment. She flopped down, her heart beating like a drum. Luke had just kissed her on the lips – OK, he hadn't meant to but . . . but . . .

She put her fingers to her mouth. She could still feel the shock that had run through her.

When Ellie emerged from her tent and went to the stables, she found Helen putting Wisp, Fizz and Milly back on the lorry, ready to drive them home to the yard – Picasso and Bill would stay on, having qualified to take part in the Supreme Ridden Pony Championship on Sunday. Helen was whistling while she worked and looked very cheerful.

'Happy birthday! Wasn't it nice of Luke to give us a lie-in?' she said. 'And he bought me some breakfast. He can be OK at times.'

Ellie smiled, her heart feeling light. 'Yeah, he can, can't he?' She had on her silver pendant. 'Look, he bought me this for my birthday and he said he'll do most of the work today.'

Helen grinned. 'So we're forgiving him then?'

Ellie nodded. 'I think we are!'

Once the ponies had been loaded up and had left, there was little for Ellie to do. She didn't ride the big hunters like Oscar and Hereward and Luke had prepared both of them, so all she had to do was help give them a final polish before Len rode them into the ring. They were lovely horses. Dapple-grey Hereward, who was in the heavyweight class, was a gentle giant at 17 hands high. Oscar, a dark bay, lightweight hunter, was smaller but very good-natured.

Oscar came seventh in his class and Hereward won – two more rosettes and another sash to decorate the lorry on its return that afternoon.

Len was in a very good mood and went off with Hereward's owners to celebrate.

Ellie headed back to the stables to muck out and prepare for the new horses who would be arriving later, but Luke was already there doing it. 'I can manage,' he told her. 'Go and chill.'

'It's OK, I really don't mind,' she said, setting to work on the box Milly had been in.

'So what do you want to do tonight?' Luke said, stopping by her stall door with a wheelbarrow. 'We could go to the disco . . . or go to the disco . . . or go to the disco!'

'Let's go to the disco then!' Ellie grinned.

'And what do you want to eat? Pizza? Burgers? Or we could get a Chinese from the takeaway and eat in the lorry?'

'Chinese,' said Ellie. She was a bit fed up with burgers and pizza now.

'Cool. Sorted!'

Luke picked up the handles of the wheelbarrow and pushed it away. Excitement flickered through Ellie at the thought of the evening ahead.

At seven o'clock, Ellie was ready. It was a warm, sultry summer night and she was wearing new denim shorts and a white top that she'd bought with some birthday money her gran had sent her. She'd had to wait for ages to use the showers, but had managed to wash her hair. It hung slightly damp in waves down her back. Her legs and arms were slim and tanned from working outside so much of the summer, but her hands felt rough from all the grooming and washing, and she had bruises on one thigh and a scratch that was healing from when she'd last fallen off Picasso. She thought of Anna's perfect legs and groaned at the comparison, but then she caught herself. After all, it wasn't as if she fancied Luke.

'No, you absolutely don't,' she reminded herself as she tried to put on some eyeshadow and mascara, using a small pocket mirror. Her blue-grey eyes stared back at her, wide and hopeful. *No, no, no*, she told herself firmly. She brushed on some lip gloss and decided she was ready.

Emerging from the tent, she went to the lorry. Luke was unpacking the boxes of Chinese from a carrier bag at the table. 'You look good,' he said, with a friendly smile.

Ellie felt awkward. He looked good too, in clean jeans and a black T-shirt, but she didn't dare say anything. For a moment she felt as if she had never been in a room with him in her life. She didn't know what to do or what to say. All she could think about was the way his hair was curling at the nape of his neck and the way he moved with easy grace, just as he rode.

'Well, don't just stand there. Help me dish this out,' said Luke, glancing round at her. 'I'm starving!'

His words brought Ellie back to reality. She went to the table and started to help him take the lids off everything. As the delicious smell wafted up, she realized how hungry she was. He'd bought crispy duck and spring rolls, spare ribs and several other dishes, as well as two pairs of chopsticks.

'Is it just for us?' said Ellie.

'Yeah, Len's eating at the pub and Helen's gone out with Cara.'

Cara was one of Len's other clients, who had also arrived that day.

'What about Anna?' said Ellie, wondering if the dark-haired girl would call in.

'She's out with her olds tonight. Some posh restaurant. They asked me to go, but I just said I was busy. I'd far rather have this with you.'

Ellie felt touched. He put some music on.

'So her parents know you're going out together now?' Ellie questioned. At first, Len had forbidden Luke to see Anna Hallett in case Jeff was annoyed – not that his words had any effect. Banning Luke from doing anything, Ellie thought, was about as pointless as trying to stop the sun coming up in the morning.

'Yeah, she told them last week. They're OK about it,' said Luke.

'You'd better not upset her, though,' said Ellie, knowing how protective Jeff Hallett was about his daughter.

'Come on, let's eat,' said Luke, changing the subject.

Luke had an enormous appetite, and as he wolfed up the food he talked about the horses and the classes that had been on that day.

Ellie found herself relaxing, drawn into the familiar conversation. They could both talk about horses without stopping and they did until all the food was gone, then they ended up sitting on the sofa together, drinking coffee and watching a video that Luke had taken on his phone of Ellie riding Milly in the show hunter pony class.

She glanced at him, 'You should have been there in the afternoon too, taken some video of Picasso.' She nudged him half accusingly.

'I know.' He pushed a hand through his hair. 'I'm

sorry. You're right. I should have been there for Picasso's class. I was a dick.' His lips curved into a hopeful smile, looking for a moment almost like a little boy. 'Have you forgiven me?'

'Hmm . . . almost.'

His grin broadened. 'You know, throwing my breeches in the bin was pretty extreme, though. I had to buy new ones today.'

She grinned too. 'I was cross with you.'

He chuckled. 'Only you could do that, Ellie. The others thought it was the best thing ever.' He put the phone down and turned to look at her. As their eyes met, Ellie felt as though she had just missed a step.

Neither of them looked away. His blue gaze seemed to draw her in, stopping her breathing.

Very slowly, he reached out and stroked her hair. She swallowed, frozen to the seat. She saw warmth flit through his eyes, then he cupped his hand round the back of her head and leant in to kiss her. Her brain felt as if it had shut down. All she knew was that she wanted to kiss him more than she wanted anything else in the world at that moment. Her lips lifted to meet his.

He kissed her gently, first her top lip, then the bottom one, before he drew back slightly. But she didn't want the space. She wanted him close, kissing her again. Her own arms reached up and curled round his neck, and then he was kissing her properly.

They pulled each other closer and closer, lips exploring, hands in each other's hair. Ellie couldn't think about anything else. Finally, they stopped and drew back. Her heart was racing so fast she thought it would burst. She saw the heat in his eyes.

'We can't.' Her voice was a whisper. 'What about Anna?'

She saw the heat cool and sense return to him. He looked at her for a moment, as if he was waking up from a dream, then he abruptly stood up and walked over to the sink, his back to her. She could see the tension in his shoulders and neck.

'Luke?' she whispered tentatively.

He cleared his throat. 'I . . . I think we should call it a night. We've got a busy day tomorrow.'

Ellie swallowed but nodded. 'Yeah.' She was feeling confused enough as it was. 'I'll see you in the morning,' she said, jumping to her feet.

'Yeah.' He still didn't quite look at her. 'See you, Ellie.'

She left the lorry, shutting the door behind her. The evening was cooler now and the breeze whispered across her hot skin. She walked in a daze to her tent and got ready for bed. When she finally lay down in her sleeping bag, she wondered what Luke was doing. What was he thinking?

She'd kissed a few boys, but it had never felt the way it had just now with Luke. It had been like being swept away, out of control, unable to stop. She'd wanted him to go on and on . . . Colour rushed into her cheeks.

'Oh no,' she groaned, rolling over and burying her hot face in her hands. Falling in love with Luke would never be a good plan, she knew that. For a start, he was going out with Anna, and second, he had made it only too clear he had no interest in a serious relationship.

'Don't fall in love with him, just don't,' Ellie pleaded with herself. But as she lay there, she had the horrible feeling that it was already too late.

Chapter Ten

When Ellie woke up the next morning, the evening before came flashing back. Feeling nervous, she pulled on her clothes and went to the stables.

Luke was tacking up Troy to work him in for the first working hunter class.

'Hi,' Ellie said, her lips feeling suddenly dry.

'Hi.' He gave her a brief smile and then busied himself with the saddle.

Ellie hesitated by the stall door, wanting to say something about the night before, but not knowing where to start. The silence stretched between them.

Luke broke it. 'I've got to bring Troy out now. Can you start on Rosie? And then when Helen comes she can do Henry. His class is after Rosie's, at about nine o'clock.'

'Sure,' Ellie said, half relieved by the normality of what he was saying, but also feeling slightly let down. Something had happened last night; something that had left her feeling the world wasn't quite the same.

She told herself to just get on with things. It was easy enough to do. All their horses entered that day had morning classes and the other horses who'd arrived the day before, like Lucifer and Gabriel, needed attention.

Anna arrived from her hotel just in time to see Luke jumping in the lightweight working hunter class with Troy. Luke was back to his best, his face utterly focused as he galloped the big bay round the course, producing a thundering clear. When he came out after doing an impressive individual show, he jumped off. Before Ellie could go over and congratulate him, Anna was at his side, putting her arms round him and kissing him. Ellie caught Luke's eye over Anna's shoulder. Emotion stabbed down inside her. She wasn't sure if it was guilt for what she'd done the night before, or jealousy or a mixture of both.

She hastily left the working hunter ring and returned to the stables. Helen was there mucking out. She didn't need much persuading to take Ellie's place at the ringside. Ellie busied herself in the stalls, but as she forked straw into the wheelbarrow she couldn't stop picturing Anna kissing Luke.

She knew she should never have kissed him the night before. He was going out with someone else. OK, he was the one who had been unfaithful, but she shouldn't have gone along with it.

And yet even as she thought that, a bit of her

wondered if maybe he would finish with Anna and ask her out instead. What would she say? *Yes!* The answer leapt inside her before she could stop it.

A little while later, Luke appeared. 'I was wondering where you'd got to,' he said as he put Troy away.

'I thought I'd give Helen a break from the mucking out. How did you do in the class in the end?'

Luke bolted Troy's door and came to the doorway, showing her a red rosette. 'Second.'

'That's brilliant!' Ellie exclaimed, stepping forward automatically to hug him but then stopping herself. She paused, the night before looming between them.

Luke saw her hesitation and took a breath. 'Um, Ellie . . . last night . . .'

'Yes?' Even she could hear the eagerness in her voice. She cursed herself. Why couldn't she just play it cool?

He bit his lip. 'It shouldn't have happened. I'm sorry.'

His words fell on her like a blow. 'Oh.' She didn't know what else to say.

He looked at the floor. 'It was stupid of me. It was just the moment. I'm way too old for you.'

'You're only three years older than me!' she protested.

'Three and a half.' His tone softened as he looked at her. 'And it's not just that. I'm not the right person for you, Ellie. I care about you, I really do, and I don't want to hurt you or mess things up. Let's just stay friends, OK? It'll be best that way.'

She gave the smallest of nods. It hurt to speak. ''K.' The sound was barely a whisper. She stared at the straw in the barrow, willing him to leave.

To her relief, he turned and walked away.

Ellie felt a lump in her throat. *I'm not going to cry over Luke, I'm not!* she thought, blinking.

Picking up the fork, she began to put straw into the barrow again, moving automatically, trying not to dwell on what had just happened and what Luke had just said.

The rest of the show passed miserably for Ellie. She knew Luke's words made sense – he was useless at relationships, and she'd only be hurt – but she couldn't stop thinking about the kiss. It had felt so right to her. If he hadn't been with Anna, maybe she would have said something more to him, tried to make him reconsider, but half the time when she saw Luke he was with the glamorous dark-haired girl, laughing, joking with her and kissing her.

Ellie knew she could never compare to Anna. She felt a longing to go home and see Spirit. Each day the walk up the hill to the stables seemed to be steeper, the ground dustier, the queuing at the shower blocks and toilets more frustrating. She just wanted the show to be over. She tried to smile when the team had wins, but she went to bed early every night to avoid seeing Anna and Luke partying together.

Saturday was the worst day when Anna rode Lucifer in the small hack class. He won his class and took the Supreme Hack Championship, leading to Jeff Hallett cracking open the champagne and offering to take all the team out for a meal at a nearby expensive restaurant. Ellie excused herself, volunteering to stay with the horses, but she still had to watch Anna and Luke kissing as they celebrated with the champagne. She lay in her tent afterwards, wishing and wishing that she was back at home.

At long last, Ellie got her desire. The show was finally over. She'd taken part in the Supreme Ridden Pony Championship although Picasso hadn't been placed, the lorries were packed up and they were on the road, heading north again. To her relief, Luke had chosen to sit in the cab with Len. Helen had gone straight to sleep in the bed over the horses. Ellie shut her eyes. All she could think about was seeing Spirit. She would feel better when she was with him. She knew she would.

It was midnight by the time she had the chance. She'd gone into the house with Len and Luke, but once they'd gone upstairs she slipped back out again with a torch. She didn't think she had ever felt more tired as she walked across the yard, her whole body aching, her heart joining in.

Breathing in the heavy smell of honeysuckle hanging in the air, she headed between the hedges that led to the fields. The stars shone out brightly in the velvet sky. She half ran up to Spirit's field, calling him in her mind. She heard his whinny and saw him canter through the darkness towards her. He stopped beside her, his coat as pale as the moon overhead.

Ellie felt unhappiness overwhelm her. Putting her arms round his neck, she burst into tears. He nuzzled her shoulder. Without her having to do anything, he saw the pictures in her head of everything that had happened that week – the joy, the unhappiness.

It's all right. You're back again now.

Ellie buried her face in his silky mane, feeling the comfort coming from him. She let her breath go. *I've missed you so much, Spirit. I really have.*

I know. I've missed you.

Her tears slowly dried. *Oh, Spirit, I wish you were still alive. I wish you could still come to shows with me just like you used to.*

You have Hope now. One day she will go to shows.

It won't be the same as you coming, Ellie replied.

There was a silence.

Have you been to see her yet?

Not really, Ellie admitted. She'd looked quickly over Hope's door when she'd been putting the horses away. The foal had been lying down. Ellie hadn't gone into her stall. She'd really just wanted to get the horses sorted and Len and Luke inside, so she could run to see Spirit as soon as possible.

She'll want to see you. She'll have missed you too.

Ellie felt a bit guilty and swiftly changed the subject. *What have you been doing while I was away? Where have you been?*

A picture of the beach and the sea filled her mind again. Spirit was standing on the sand and staring out across the water. Was it her imagination or was the pull from the land on the other side stronger than last time he had shown her the image? She frowned as she sensed another emotion coming from him as he stood there on the beach. What was it?

You feel lonely?

Yes. Spirit sent her a memory of himself grazing in the fields with the other horses before he died. *I miss them. I miss being around other horses.*

Ellie stroked his neck not knowing quite what to say. She had never thought about Spirit missing the other horses, but of course he would. When he'd been alive, he'd loved nothing more than being out in the field with his friends. *Can't you be with the horses in the field now? Can't you join them?*

They cannot see or hear me when I am invisible. Only you can.

Ellie bit her lip. *Oh.* She hated the idea of Spirit longing for horse company. But what could she do? Unless . . .

She stopped her train of thought there. No, it was a solution, but she wouldn't even consider it. She and Spirit were going to be together forever.

I love you, Spirit, she thought, resting her head against his neck.

She felt the love coming from him in return, enveloping her. Overhead, a dark cloud drifted over the moon.

The next day, Ellie was up at 7 a.m., straight back into the usual yard routine. Luke had been given the day off and had left to spend it with Anna. The horses who had been at the show the last few days were being rested, so Ellie used the extra time to catch up with the horses she hadn't seen. Remembering what Spirit had said, she went to see Hope first thing. However, the little foal was nowhere near as welcoming as Spirit. She butted her head hard against Ellie's stomach when Ellie went into her stall.

'Steady!' Ellie gasped as Hope gave her a sharp nip, as if in punishment for deserting her. 'Hope, don't do that!'

The filly turned her back on her.

'Come here, silly!' Ellie said, walking to her head and trying to hug her, but the filly turned away again. Ellie moved after her, but once again Hope swung round.

Ellie felt a prickle of disappointment that the foal

wasn't more pleased to see her. 'All right, be like that!' she said, half-exasperated.

After helping with the feeds, she went to check on Lexi and Rocky in the other barn. Lexi was looking good. Stuart had told her the physio had been a few times and Lexi seemed to be responding well to treatment. Ellie stroked the grey mare. Even in just a week she could feel Lexi was so much more relaxed and happy.

She wished she could say the same about Rocky. When she went to his stall that morning, he looked tense and anxious. He jumped to the back of his stall, his head high, the whites of his eyes showing as he watched her warily. She remembered how quiet he had seemed when he has first arrived.

'What's up with Rocky?' Ellie called to Stuart, who was across the aisle checking the water buckets.

'He's been like this all week,' Stuart replied. 'I don't know why. No one's done anything to him. I tried moving him from the courtyard to this stable in here to see if it would help, but it's not made a blind bit of difference. Sasha won't go in his stall now – he took a chunk out of her arm on Tuesday when she went in with the feedbucket. Watch yourself if you have to go in for any reason, particularly if you're carrying a bucket.'

Ellie frowned. 'Can I spend a bit of time with him this morning, Stu?'

'I was hoping you'd offer. See if you can work your usual magic.'

Stuart left her to it. Ellie thought about what he'd just said. Most horses wouldn't attack you when you had a feed for them; it was usually when they were at their most affectionate so what had made Rocky go for Sasha? And why had he become so anxious? Neither Sasha nor Stuart would have hurt him in any way. What had caused the change in him in the last week?

She opened her mind to him. *You can talk to me if you want*, she thought gently. *Tell me what's wrong.*

But, just as before, she had the distinct feeling he was throwing up a wall between them.

Ellie sent the horse waves of reassurance and love, telling him over and over again that there was no need for him to be afraid of her. Then she opened the door. Rocky didn't try and bite her, but he turned his back on her, one back hoof stamping down threateningly. She hesitated but decided that taking little steps might be the answer. She would be patient and wait.

'You're safe here,' she murmured, wishing she could make him believe it. 'And when you're ready to talk, I'll be listening.'

He turned to watch her as she left the stall.

'Any luck?' Stuart called from the water tap as she walked down the yard.

'Sorry,' Ellie replied. 'I think we'll just have to give him a bit more time.'

Stuart nodded. 'OK. Can you groom Barney? His new owners are coming to pick him up later.'

Ellie's heart sank. 'Already?'

'Yes.' Stuart saw her face. 'But he's going to a good home – so don't be too upset.'

Even knowing he was leaving for a good home, Ellie still felt her heart wrench as Barney walked into the trailer, his chestnut coat shining in the sun. His ears were pricked as he pulled cheekily at the T-shirt that Alex, his new owner, was wearing. He seemed to think he was just off to a horse show. *Where are we going this time?* he seemed to say.

'Bye, boy,' Ellie murmured, feeding him a last mint when he was tied up inside the trailer. She turned to Alex. 'Make sure you always lock and bolt his stable door and tie him up with a double knot. He's a complete Houdini.'

She remembered the time when she first arrived at High Peak Stables and Joe had said the same words to her. She wished Joe could be there to say goodbye to Barney too, but maybe it was easier for him that he wasn't.

'Thanks, any other tips?' twelve-year-old Alex asked eagerly.

'No, just give him lots of hugs and he'll be happy.'

Alex smiled. 'Oh, I think I can manage that,' she said, kissing Barney's neck and ruffling his mane. 'We're going to have so much fun together, aren't we, boy?'

Barney snorted all over her and she giggled. Ellie left the trailer, feeling slightly better but still sad.

Bye, Barney, she thought as she stood with Len watching the trailer bump off down the drive.

'Now *that* was a good sale,' Len said, patting the cheque in his pocket.

Ellie felt a wave of dislike. The money was all that mattered to him.

'I imagine we'll have some offers flooding in for Picasso after the win last week.' Len smiled with satisfaction. 'Time for him to move on too. You can concentrate on the youngsters.'

Ellie couldn't bear the thought of saying goodbye to Picasso as well as Barney, or hearing her uncle talking as if the horses were just cars or something inanimate he was selling. 'I'm going up to the fields.'

'What? To hang around that grave some more?' Len's eyes narrowed.

Ellie shrugged, trying to stay calm and not react.

Len shook his head. 'You spend far too much bloody time there as it is. Go back on the yard and bring Gem out instead.'

'I just want ten minutes!' Ellie said.

Her uncle's expression darkened. 'Let's have none of your arguments now. Just do as I say.'

'No!' Ellie retorted. For a long time she'd had to do what her uncle said because she knew if she really angered him he might not let Spirit stay on the yard, but now he didn't have that hold on her. Hope wasn't the same as Spirit. If her uncle threatened to throw her off the yard . . . well, she would deal with it.

'I'm taking a break,' she said, refusing to be intimidated. 'Luke, Stuart, Helen, Sasha – they all have breaks and days off. I work just as hard as them. I'm going to take ten minutes!' She marched past him.

Len grabbed her arm, his other hand raising.

At the feel of his fingers on her arm, Ellie's temper snapped and she turned on him like a wild cat, all the frustration of the last months bursting out. 'Let me go!' she hissed. 'If you lay a finger on me – I'll report you!'

For a moment they stared furiously at each other. But then her uncle's grip slowly released. 'Ten minutes. No more!' he snapped.

Ellie walked away, her head spinning. She'd stood up to her uncle and won. She couldn't quite believe it. She broke into a run as she reached the fields and raced up the hill to the peace of Spirit's grave.

Chapter Eleven

'Third time lucky!' Ellie muttered to herself as she picked herself off the schooling ring floor and dusted down her jodhpurs, though she didn't know why she was bothering. She was bound to be thrown off again. Her uncle was getting his own back for her earlier rebellion by making her ride one of the newly backed young horses. She wished he could have chosen Solo or Maestro, both of them started by Joe with gentle methods before he'd left for Canada, but her uncle had decided to put her on a particularly stubborn dun filly called Sandy. Every time Len legged Ellie back into the saddle, the filly started bucking.

'We haven't got all day!' Len snapped as Ellie walked slowly back to Sandy who was looking at her smugly. 'Legs down, hang on to the neck strap and don't let her throw you off this time.'

'Maybe we could start her by using join-up, like Joe did with Solo and Maestro,' said Ellie, her elbows scraped, her back aching.

Len fixed her with a hard look. 'Maybe you could stop talking and just stay on!'

Gritting her teeth, Ellie put her hand on the saddle, lifting her left leg for a leg up. The instant she was on, she found her stirrups and grabbed the neck strap as she felt the filly hump her back. *Here we go!* she thought with a gasp.

Sandy threw her head down and kicked her heels up, but this time Ellie was ready. Clinging like a limpet, she stuck on four enormous bronco bucks at which point the filly stopped and looked round at her, surprised, as if to say, *Are you still there?*

'Oh, yes,' Ellie told her, 'I'm here.' She rewarded the pony with a pat for standing still and not bucking.

'We're not done yet,' Len grunted. 'Let's have her walking.'

Sandy had several more bucking fits, but each time Ellie was ready and stayed on. Soon the pony gave in and by the end of the session Ellie had her walking and trotting round. Not that her uncle seemed pleased. He simply opened the gate for her without saying a word as she rode through.

Ellie hosed Sandy down, every bone in her body sore. Not for the first time, she longed for Joe to be there to talk to. He'd have understood. She thought about what he might be doing now in Canada. Probably just getting up. She wondered if he'd have bought a Stetson hat like the one his new boss, Ray, wore, and cheered herself up by smiling at the thought of Joe in a Stetson and cowboy boots.

Luke didn't come home until very late that night. Ellie woke as she heard his motorbike, and stretched her aching limbs. She turned over in bed but couldn't sleep. Her thoughts seemed to be jumping from one thing to another – her uncle, Luke and, most of all, Spirit. His words from yesterday had been haunting her. She hated the thought of him being lonely and unhappy, missing the company of other horses as well as missing her when she wasn't there.

I'll just have to spend more time with him, she thought. It would be hard; there was never much opportunity for sneaking off, but she would do everything she could.

'So what's up with you and Len?' Luke said the next morning. 'You're barely speaking to each other. What's going on?'

'We had an argument yesterday,' Ellie admitted. 'Then he put me on Sandy and I fell off. She went nuts, broncoing and everything.'

'You must really have annoyed him if he put you on her. Didn't you hear she had Stuart off twice last week, and he can stay on anything?'

Ellie raised her eyebrows. 'No, he didn't tell me that.' Still, she couldn't help feeling a flicker of pleasure that she'd managed to stay on Sandy in the end.

'Don't get on Len's bad side, Ellie,' Luke warned. 'Just do what he wants, don't argue.'

She frowned. 'You argue with him.'

'Yeah, well, I'm me. Don't you do it.'

She saw the concern in his eyes and looked away. She almost preferred it when Luke was being annoying. When he was caring, she found it even harder to be around him without wishing that things had turned out very differently after the kiss.

For a moment Luke looked as if he would say something more, but then he turned. 'Right, better get on. Anna's coming later to see Lucifer and Rocky.'

'Great!' Ellie muttered as Luke strode away down the yard.

Ellie spent as much time as she could at Spirit's grave that day to avoid being on the yard with Luke and Anna. She felt a bit guilty, knowing she could be working with Hope. But the foal was still being stand-offish with her, refusing to be hugged and turning away. Spirit, in contrast was always delighted to see her.

The week went by and Ellie found herself visiting Spirit more and more. They would stand and talk in the days, and in the evenings she would sit on his back and they'd go out into the woods. She felt so much happier when she was with him than on the yard. Her uncle was still angry with her and spending time with Spirit meant she could avoid being with him – and seeing Luke. The only downside was that being with Spirit meant having less time to spend trying to listen to and heal the other horses on the yard.

On Thursday afternoon, she was just about to visit Spirit again when Len called to her, a bridle and saddle in his arms. 'It's time to try out this new horse of the Halletts. We need to start him being ridden so Anna can get on him. Come and help me in the school.'

'You're getting on Rocky?' Ellie frowned. She'd had no luck so far with Anna's new horse. He'd refused to talk to her and although he would now let her into his stable, she could tell he didn't want her to touch him or to let her anywhere near him. 'I don't think he's ready to be ridden yet.'

Len's eyebrows shot up his forehead. 'Oh, really?'

Ellie felt a wave of dislike. 'No, I don't. I think there's something wrong with him.'

'The only thing wrong with him is he's in that stable guzzling hay and feed and not doing any work. I'm getting on him.'

'I really don't think it's a good idea,' Ellie insisted.

'Well, I do, and though you seem to be forgetting it, what I say goes around here!' Len strode to the barn.

Dread gripped Ellie. She was sure, utterly sure, that Len shouldn't try riding Rocky. But what could she do? She couldn't even ask one of the others to stop him. Stuart was out on a hack with Luke, it was Sasha's day off, and Helen had gone to the feed shop.

Len led Rocky out of the stable. Already the horse's neck was sweating and he looked scared.

'Don't ride him!' Ellie's anger faded as her fear intensified. She could feel the waves of stress coming from the horse.

Ignoring her, Len led Rocky up to the school, the bay jogging and pulling anxiously. 'Walk on, you daft thing!' Len growled.

He opened the gate and pulled down the stirrups. With a quick spring, he was sitting down in the saddle. Ellie saw all Rocky's muscles tense and then he simply exploded. He went berserk, shooting round the ring, his head down between his knees, his legs kicking up in a twisting series of bucks. She'd thought Sandy was a bucker, but she was nothing compared to Rocky. He jackknifed in the air, plunging and kicking, his eyes rolling as he did everything in his power to be free of the weight on his back.

Len was a very experienced horseman, but not even a rodeo rider could have stayed on. Ellie saw him fall forward heavily on to Rocky's neck, losing his reins and balance. Rocky plunged his head down again and twisted his back legs up near the fence.

The movement dislodged Len and he was flung through the air, crashing into a fence post and thumping down to the ground.

Ellie froze. Rocky bucked twice more, his reins and stirrups flapping, and then realizing he was free, he trotted to the far side of the school.

Get up! Get up! Ellie thought, but her uncle didn't move. Hands shaking, she pulled herself over the gate and ran across the schooling ring towards him. She gave a muffled gasp. Blood was running down the side of his face and pooling under his still head . . .

Chapter Twelve

Ellie stared at her uncle lying on the ground. 'Uncle Len?'

He didn't move.

Was he dead?

No, she could see his chest was still moving. But he was unconscious. What should she do? She knew you shouldn't move someone if they were badly injured in case they had damaged their spine or neck.

Phone an ambulance. Reaching into her pocket with trembling fingers Ellie pulled out her phone and punched in 999.

'Which service do you require?' said a voice.

'Ambulance!' she gasped. It only took a second for her to be put through and then she was talking to a calm woman who asked her lots of questions about where she was and what had happened and took her phone number. 'We're sending someone now,' said the woman. 'It'll be an air ambulance. Is there anyone with you?'

'No. I can ring them, though. They're nearby.' Ellie felt an overwhelming longing to speak to Luke, to hear his voice, to have him tell her it would be all right.

'Ring them. I'll call you back in a moment.'

Everything happened so fast. The bright red helicopter was there within five minutes, before Luke and Stuart had even returned home. Having been told by the lady on the phone not to move her uncle in any way, Ellie put Rocky in his stable before the helicopter arrived. She was very glad she'd thought of it. The horses in the fields charged around in alarm as it landed, its rotors whirring.

The pilot and two other paramedics in orange suits jumped out, and quickly started dealing with Len.

One of them, a lady called Pat, stood with Ellie, explaining what was happening. They were all very efficient and calm. It felt unreal to Ellie, like being part of a TV show, as she watched her uncle being stabilized and strapped on to a fluorescent yellow board. 'Now, do you want to come with us?' Pat asked as Len was lifted carefully into the helicopter.

'I-I can't,' Ellie stammered. 'I shouldn't leave here.'

To her relief, just then she caught sight of Luke and Stuart galloping along the drive on Oscar and Zak, heedless of the horses' legs.

It seemed only seconds before Luke was running

up the hill to the schooling ring. 'Ellie!' He grabbed her and pulled her close. Feeling his arms round her, her composure disintegrated and she started to cry.

'I'm Len's nephew,' Luke explained to the paramedic over her head. 'What's happening?'

Pat explained and told Luke where the ambulance was going. 'One of you can come with us or you could meet us at the hospital.'

'We'll meet you there,' said Luke. 'We'll come in the car.'

'Is Uncle Len going to be all right?' Ellie asked fearfully.

'We need to take him to hospital to find out for sure what the matter is. The wound on his head isn't serious, though. It's more a case of what other damage he's done. We won't know until he's had a full body X-ray and CT scan.' Pat gave her a sympathetic look. 'You did all you could by calling the ambulance as quickly as you did.'

Not all I could, thought Ellie. *I should have stopped him riding Rocky. Or sorted Rocky out before he rode him.* She felt a guilty lurch as she realized that she might have found out what was the matter with Rocky if she hadn't been spending so much time with Spirit.

Pat and the other paramedics got into the ambulance, gave a wave and then shut the door. Ellie and Luke watched as the rotors turned faster and it rose into the sky. Stuart had joined them at the gate. His face was etched with worry. 'What happened?' he said to Ellie.

'You can tell us in the kitchen,' said Luke. 'Let's get you a cup of sweet tea, that's good for shock.'

Ellie nodded, her legs trembling. As she turned to walk out of the school, they gave way. Luke caught her and scooped her up in his arms as if she weighed nothing. Ellie was too shocked even to struggle. She rested her head against his chest, giving in for the moment to being looked after. 'Come on. Let's take you inside,' he said.

Once she was sitting in the kitchen with a cup of tea, Ellie's trembling calmed and she told Stuart and Luke about the way Rocky had gone mad. 'No one could have stayed on.' She shook her head. 'I tried to stop Len riding him. I should have tried harder.'

'It's not your fault.' Luke squeezed her hands tightly. 'Don't even begin to think that.'

'Luke's right. No one can stop Len when he's a mind to do something,' Stuart agreed. 'You know that only too well. Sounds as if we don't know everything about Rocky's past, though. Horses don't behave like that without a reason. I'll get it checked out.'

Elllie felt slightly better.

'We should get changed and find some things for Len, then drive to the hospital,' Luke said. Pat had told them there was no rush. Len would need to have his injuries assessed and then go into the operating theatre. There would be a lot of waiting around to hear news.

Ellie stood up. 'You're not going to collapse again, are you?' Luke said.

'No.' She managed a shaky smile. 'Thanks, Luke.'

'Come on, let's get moving,' he said.

Pat, the paramedic, had been right. There *was* a lot of waiting around. In the end, the news came through and it was reasonably good. Although Len had concussed himself, bruised a couple of ribs, fractured the femur in his left leg and badly sprained his right ankle, his neck and back – the two areas that the paramedics had been most worried about – were fine. He'd be in hospital for a week or so and then walking on crutches, but the doctors were hopeful he would make a full recovery. By the time Ellie and Luke went into see him he had regained consciousness, but was now sedated in intensive care.

'It will seem as if he's asleep, but he's only just under the surface. A lot of patients do recall their family talking to them while they were sedated, so if you want to speak to him, then do,' the staff nurse in charge of Len explained.

It was strange seeing Len looking so vulnerable with his eyes closed. There were tubes coming from all over him and a breathing piece attached to his mouth, which went to a ventilator working his lungs. He was tucked in under white sheets, his hands and arms on the outside. His weather-beaten face looked grey, his eyes shut, and his wrinkles seemed deeper then ever. Ellie stared at him, not knowing quite how she felt.

Guilty, yes. Even though she accepted what Luke and Stuart said about there being no way she could have stopped Len, she still felt guilty she hadn't tried harder with Rocky that week. She'd told herself she was giving him time, but deep down, in her heart of hearts, she knew she could have spent more time with him than she had.

So yes, guilty. And sorry for her uncle lying there in hospital injured, but that was about it. She couldn't love him just because he was injured. She edged towards the window, wishing they could leave. There were six beds in the intensive care unit and there were patients in each of them, who were connected to machines like Len was. Ellie glanced out at the sky and longed to be away, back in the fresh air. Another wave of guilt hit her that she didn't feel more upset.

Luke sat beside Len on a chair and held his hand. 'Don't worry about a thing, Len,' he was saying. 'I'll see to everything. Just get better. The yard will run fine until you come home.'

He sat there talking for what seemed a very long time to Ellie, but Len didn't move or even stir. In the end, the nurse came and told them it might be best if they left for the day. 'I'll come again tomorrow,' Luke told Len. 'Just recover and don't worry about anything.'

'Do you think he could hear you like the nurse said?' Ellie asked as they left and walked down the echoing corridor, away from the bleeping, whirring machines.

'I don't know, but it made me feel better saying it to him and if he could hear, well, hopefully, it's made him feel better too.'

Ellie nodded. They drove home in silence. It was almost dark when they arrived. 'I'll stick on some supper,' said Luke as they left the car.

'I'll check round the horses,' Ellie offered. She went from stall to stall, making sure water buckets were filled, straightening rugs, re-hanging haynets. She liked doing the last check of the night. The horses were always calm and relaxed then, many of them lying down, most greeting her with low pleased whickers.

Not Rocky. He shot to the back of his stall when she opened the door.

'Oh, Rocky, what has happened to you in the past?' Ellie whispered. The horse stared at her fearfully. Ellie was tempted to try connecting with him again, but she felt drained and exhausted and communicating with reluctant horses took a lot of energy. She knew she should wait until she was feeling stronger herself. *Tomorrow*, she decided.

Leaving the barn, she went to the field. Spirit came to her as soon as she called. She told him all about the day.

I just feel so bad I haven't connected with Rocky yet.

Spirit nuzzled her. *You have been spending a lot of time here with me. Maybe you should come here less often.*

No! I don't want you to be lonely.

I know and I don't want to see you less, but the living need you more than I do.

But I *need* you, *Spirit*, Ellie told him, twining her hands in his mane. She struggled to put her feelings into words. *All the rest of the time – when I'm not with you – it's as if I'm just pretending, getting through the time until I can be here with you, in my real life.*

But this isn't *your real life, Ellie.* She felt a deep sadness coming from him. For a moment she had the unnerving sensation of holding water in her hands, trying to stop it draining away through her fingers.

But she was too tired to think about it any more just then. *Let's not talk about this now.*

Yes.

He nuzzled her and putting her forehead against his, she let the world fade away.

Ellie sent Joe an email telling him what had happened: *They say he'll be OK*, she finished. *Only, Joe, I wish you were here. E xx*

She slept fitfully that night. Luke went back to the hospital in the morning. He asked if she wanted to go, but when she gave a feeble excuse about staying with the horses he seemed to understand.

Later that day, Joe rang. 'I've just seen your email. How's Dad?'

'He's going to be OK,' Ellie said, pressing the phone close to her ear, wishing Joe was there next to her. 'Luke went to the hospital this morning and is still there now. They think your dad'll be in hospital for a week, then when he comes out he'll be on crutches for a while and not able to move much.'

Joe whistled through his teeth. 'He'll hate that.'

'I know.' Ellie couldn't begin to imagine how someone as active and physical as her uncle would react to being so restricted.

'I want to come home,' said Joe. 'Just for a visit – to see him and help out on the yard. You'll all be really up against it without Dad and it's the busiest time of year.'

'You can't fly all the way back here,' protested Ellie, but she felt a flicker of hope inside.

'I can,' said Joe. 'I talked to Ray as soon as I saw your mail. He said it's fine and that of course I can come. I'll check the times when I get a ticket and text you later.'

'You're really coming back?' said Ellie, shutting her eyes and praying he meant it. She realized she so desperately wanted to see his familiar face and smile, to feel him hugging her.

'I'll be there as soon as I can.'

Clicking the END CALL button, Ellie felt as if a weight had lifted from her shoulders. It would be brilliant to have Joe back, even if just for a while. It was less than two months since he'd left, but it felt like forever. So much had happened in that time – Spirit dying, all the shows, Luke and her . . .

No! Ellie stopped her thoughts there. There was no 'Luke and her'.

Feeling cross with herself, she walked up the yard.

Chapter Thirteen

Ellie texted Luke to tell him Joe was coming home and then she told Stuart, Helen and Sasha. They were all delighted at the news; Joe was so easygoing and helpful. He'd always put himself out for people and he was such a part of the yard. Ellie realized how much everyone had been missing him.

Maybe he'll stay . . .

The thought jumped across her mind as she groomed Lexi that afternoon. She felt torn. Joe was having a great time in Canada. From his emails she knew he loved learning how to use natural horsemanship techniques, being on a yard where they used them every day and were open to new methods. She also knew he'd been having fun – he was always telling her about the barbecues he went to, the parties at people's houses. He'd been so under Len's thumb and worked so hard when he lived at the yard that he'd never had time for going out. She wanted him back at the stables, but she also wanted him to be happy.

She patted the grey mare, who nuzzled her affectionately. 'It's all so complicated, Lexi,' Ellie sighed.

'Ellie!'

Hearing Stuart's voice, she looked round. 'I'm in here!' she called.

Stuart's face was serious as he came to the door. 'You know I said I'd try to find out about Rocky?'

She nodded.

'Well, I have. A mate of mine used to work at the yard where Rocky came from. He's left now. Couldn't stick it any longer.'

'Why?' Looking at Stuart's face, Ellie felt a cold dread in her stomach. 'I thought it was a yard where they have good show results.'

'It is, but they don't get those results in good ways.' Stuart shook his head. 'Seems like they weren't exactly truthful about Rocky's history.'

Ellie dread deepened. 'What did they do to him?'

'My friend says that when Rocky arrived he was really stubborn and resistant, and when they tried to break him in he fought them so the yard owner, Bill, shut him away in a stable. He wasn't allowed out. Wasn't given any food or water until he was weakened, then food or water was never left with him, but he always had to take it from one of the grooms who would carry a bucket in.'

'But that's awful!' Ellie burst out.

Stuart rubbed his bald head. 'Awful but not

unusual. You break the horse's spirit by taking away all it needs – light, space, food, water – you bring it down physically and then you break it in when it's too damn scared and weak to fight you.'

Ellie swallowed. Now she was beginning to see why Rocky was throwing up such barriers against communication. He must fear all humans.

'Apparently, Rocky was a hard case to crack – even when he was weak he still fought. My friend left before Rocky did, but he reckons given the timescale of when Jeff Hallett bought him and the fact he doesn't look half starved, Bill would have decided to cut his losses, fatten him up and then dope him in order to sell him.'

'Saying he was quiet as a donkey,' said Ellie, remembering the words of the groom who had dropped Rocky off. She remembered touching Rocky the day he'd arrived and the sense of fog she'd felt from him. He'd been drugged! That explained why his behaviour had grown worse over the next few days as the drugs had worn off.

Stuart shook his head. 'I don't know what we're going to do. It'll be no easy feat to deal with him now, after that start. Jeff Hallett won't be pleased. I guess when he finds out he'll demand his money back from Bill.'

'But that would mean Rocky returning to the same yard!' Ellie couldn't let that happen. She wouldn't. She'd throw herself in front of the horsebox before it did. 'Stu, I might be able to do something with Rocky now I know all this.' Her eyes pleaded with him. 'Let me try. Len won't be back for a few weeks. Luke won't care. Let's just tell Jeff we're working on him and taking it slowly. He's not expecting him to be ready for showing until next year anyway. Please?'

Stuart thought about it for a few moments and then nodded. 'I don't want to send him back to a place like that either, if you can do something – do.'

Relief rushed through her.

'I'll leave him to you then,' Stuart said. 'I don't know what you do, but I do know you have a knack with horses like him. Be careful though. It's not worth getting injured for.'

Ellie nodded. She'd no idea what she would do. She'd already tried communicating with Rocky and had got nowhere, but now she was determined to keep trying. She wouldn't let him be sent back.

Ellie put the grooming kit away in the tackroom. She'd been hoping to see Spirit after she'd groomed Lexi. With Luke and Len not around and three of the livery horses to prepare for a show the next day, she hadn't had a chance to visit his grave all day. She hesitated. She wanted to see him, he'd be missing her, but Rocky needed her too.

And Hope, she admitted guiltily. She hadn't had time to do anything with the foal other than put her out in the field with Gem. The little foal's manners were getting worse – she was starting to barge around when she was led and refusing to lift her feet up for Ellie to pick out her hooves. Ellie felt slightly confused at her own behaviour if she was honest. She'd been so keen to buy Hope, but since she'd bought her and got back from the Royal International she'd done nothing with her really. *It's just cos I've been so busy*, she told herself. *It won't harm her to just go out in the field with Gem. I can start training her more in a while.*

Ellie now looked towards the field with Spirit's grave in, pulled in different directions. Spirit needed her and she wanted to be there, but the words he had spoken to her came back into her head: *The living need you more than I do.*

She sighed. Rocky really *did* need her. Trying to ignore the pull of Spirit's grave, she went to the barn where the young bay was stabled.

As usual, he hunched himself up in a corner when she came to the door, his eyes scared, his muscles tense, his beautiful head to the wall. She could feel how much he wanted to run away from her.

Ellie let herself into the stable, watching him closely. If he tried to go for her, she would have to get out. But the horse didn't move.

Ellie took a breath and shut her eyes.

Breathing deeply in and out, she cleared her mind, emptying all thoughts of Luke, Len, Joe, Hope, even

Spirit. All she thought about was the frightened horse in front of her. Love and the desire to help welled up as she opened her mind and sensed the familiar barrier around him.

Let me in, she thought patiently. *I only want to help, Rocky. I know what's happened to you.*

How could she get through to him? Acting on her instincts, she sent him pictures of what Stuart had told her – she imagined a stable, imagined feeling confined, hungry, thirsty, scared; having no water, no food; growing weaker . . .

She heard a movement in the straw and opened her eyes. Rocky had turned towards her. He was staring at her as if he'd picked up on her thoughts.

'It's OK,' she whispered. 'I know about it.' Thinking about how he must feel, about how humans had been the aggressors in his life, she took a risk and sank down on the straw and pulled her knees to her chest, making herself small. Then shutting her eyes, she imagined the hunger and thirst again, and over it she sent all the love and understanding she could.

Very slowly, she felt a change in the atmosphere in the stable. It was as though the barrier between them was slowly starting to melt.

The straw rustled. She sensed movement and knew he was coming towards her, but she didn't open her eyes. Giving the horse her trust, she stayed still as she felt him approach. She was at his mercy sitting there. He could do anything, kick her, bite her . . .

Warm breath blew over her fingers. She opened her eyes and saw that his muzzle was by her hands. She stared into his dark eyes and for a moment felt lost in time and space. Very slowly, she reached out and touched the centre of his forehead, her hand cupped, resting as lightly on him as a leaf floating on a stream. The doors opened suddenly between them, the walls falling down and their minds connecting. In a single second it seemed as if a thousand thoughts passed between them. Ellie had never felt such a rush of feelings and images. She let everything flow through her and felt a huge sense of release as Rocky suddenly sighed deeply.

For a long moment Ellie just sat there. She'd never felt anything like this before. To go from no connection to suddenly feeling everything . . . she waited, letting the energy settle, sensing Rocky slowly relax. The air seemed to grow heavy and still around them and then she heard his voice in her head.

Why did they do it?

Ellie had been asked that question by horses before. Once again, she had no real answer as she sensed his confusion and bewilderment. *Because . . . because that's just the way some humans behave to horses. But not here. You're safe here. Tell me about what happened to you.*

She saw into his memories. The stable was even

smaller than she'd imagined it, completely dark with no windows, the top door shut and bolted. She could feel Rocky's terrible hunger; the thirst raging through him; the fear every time the door opened, and then the growing hatred of the humans who would only let him eat and drink from the buckets they were holding. She could feel his body weakening and then she became him as one day he was led to the ring, legs and body weak, eyes hurting in the strong sunlight. She saw the two men approaching, one with a lunge whip, one with a riding hat who mounted. Half-starved and dehydrated, she felt the fear and fury surge through Rocky in equal measures. Bucking and kicking, he threw the weight from his body and then turned on the man in the centre, chasing him across the school until the man escaped by throwing himself over the fence.

He snorted softly and she sent him waves of love and comfort.

Oh, Rocky. It won't happen here. Don't be scared any more. Don't hate. You have to let people ride you or you'll be sold, but you'll go out in the fields, you'll eat freely, drink fresh water. She sent him pictures of being out in the sunny fields, of him trotting happily around the schooling ring carrying a rider, of big haynets and buckets of fresh water. Then she stood up, wanting to heal his unhappiness. With one hand on his chest and another on his back, she watched his face as she let healing energy flow. His head dropped low, his eyes half closing. He licked and chewed with his mouth.

Lost in what she was doing, Ellie moved around his body, placing her hands where she sensed it would help. Rocky swayed gently from side to side, completely relaxed now.

When she sensed he had had enough, she returned to his head and placed her hand on his forehead once more. She felt his new happiness, calmness, balance. Taking her hand away, she stepped back. Rocky blinked and slowly raised his head, looking slightly dazed as if he had been asleep. He looked at her and then stepped forward and nuzzled his face against her.

Ellie rubbed his neck, happiness welling inside her as she saw the trust in his eyes. She'd thought it would take her ages to work with him, but that was the thing about communicating with horses in the way she did. She could never predict how long it would take to help them: some would need patience and time; others, like Rocky, could be helped in a single session. She could sense how much Rocky had wanted to be rid of the fear and confusion, so much so that once he had put his trust in her, he had been prepared to let her help him as much as she could.

'You're so brave,' she whispered, smoothing his forelock and realizing what a special horse he was. 'Thank you for letting me in.'

She was suddenly overwhelmed by the sense that this was where she was meant to be, what she was meant to be doing with her life and joy bubbled up through her. But then an image crossed her mind. A grey horse standing on a hillside. *Spirit.*

Ellie felt as if cold water had washed all over her. She couldn't be healing horses and be with Spirit. Yes, she could go between the two, but she knew what the pull was like to be with Spirit, how it had taken a horse as badly in need as Rocky to make her turn away from his grave that day. It would have been fine if she had empty days, but she didn't. There was always so much to do on the yard – people needing her to do this, that and the other – and now it was the summer holidays. Her time would become even more stretched when she was back at school.

But what can I do? she thought helplessly. *I can't give up either thing.* She looked at Rocky, now standing half asleep beside her, and felt again the joy and fulfilment of making him better. But then she thought of Spirit again and experienced the familiar longing for him. She wanted to see him, stroke him, talk to him – he was her horse and she loved him more than anything in the world. When she was with him, she felt happy and at peace, as if he had never died.

What *could* she do?

She swallowed. There was no easy answer.

Chapter Fourteen

You did so well.

Ellie stood stroking Spirit's mane. It was dusk, the sky deepening to a dark grey, the first few stars shining out. *His fear, his hunger and thirst – it was awful, Spirit.*

Spirit breathed on her hands. *But you helped him.*

I was so glad I could. Ellie remembered the feeling of fulfilment, but as she thought about it she also remembered the way she had felt so torn. She didn't want Spirit to see her thoughts. But it was too late.

He sent the feelings back to her – the doubts, the confusion, the feeling of being pulled in two ways – with a question. *You felt like that?*

Lying wasn't possible. *Yes. Only for a moment, though. It's just hard finding time for everything sometimes.* She tried to smile. *But though I like helping horses, I want to be here, with you. That's the most important thing.*

She reached for Spirit's thoughts, wondering how

he was feeling; hoping he wasn't hurt by her admittance. But all she found was a quiet thoughtfulness.

Maybe there's a reason why the dead don't come back.

Ellie felt her stomach clench and suddenly she was scared of where the conversation was heading. She changed the subject.

Should . . . should we go for a ride?

Spirit snorted softly. *Yes.*

Was it her imagination or had she picked up relief from him at the change of subject too?

She vaulted on to his back and they set out into the woods. It was a quiet ride. Neither of them spoke much to each other. Ellie felt as though her thoughts were swirling, grabbing at her, trying to be heard, but she pushed them determinedly away.

We're here together now, she reminded herself. *That's all that matters. Walk in the present, remember?*

She focused on the feel of Spirit's warm back beneath her, the feel of his silky mane in her fingers, and tried not to think about anything else.

The next morning, Ellie heard from Joe, saying that he'd booked a flight and would arrive in two days' time on Monday afternoon. She was longing to see him. Luke seemed to be avoiding her. Whenever she went into the feedroom or tackroom, he always found an excuse to leave and he never once suggested they hack out together. Ellie missed the closeness they'd had. She'd grown used to him teasing her, talking to her, discussing the horses with her. There weren't even any shows to bring them together. With Len out of action, Stuart had cancelled all the show trips apart from the ones where clients' horses were entered.

Ellie tried to spend more time with the foal. Hope was still misbehaving, pulling away and striking out with her small front hooves when she was led, nipping with her sharp teeth when told off. Ellie decided to work with her in the schooling ring, setting out a grid of poles to walk her through and around. It was a training method that Joe had told her about to encourage cooperation and obedience. It involved working the horse by using voice commands and signals made with a long whip, although the whip was never used to hit the horse.

Ellie read up on it, but the first time she tried it with Hope she found that it seemed much easier in theory than practice. The filly barged into her, tripping over the poles, and refusing to listen to her voice commands 'walk' and 'whoa'. She took absolutely no notice of the whip. The book had said that when placed across the horse's chest it would help stop the horse. Hope just walked straight on through it.

Ellie's frustration grew. All the time the filly was messing around was time she could have spent with Spirit. Finally, she was so cross, she shouted at her, banging the end of the whip down on the floor in front of Hope's nose.

Quick as a flash, the filly grabbed the stick, pulled it out of Ellie's hands and tossed it over her shoulder across the school.

'Now that's an interesting training method, Ellie,' Luke's voice came from the gate. He had paused there with a wheelbarrow. 'So you teach the horse to hold the whip now, do you?'

'Oh, shut up!' Ellie groaned.

Hearing his familiar infuriating chuckle for the first time in days, she stomped over to pick up the whip. She'd wanted Luke to start talking to her again, but not like this. She glanced up, but he'd already gone on his way. Shaking her head, she turned back to Hope. The filly gave her a smug look.

'Oh, I give up!' said Ellie. 'You can go back in your field.'

Hope jogged beside her and nipped at her all the way down to the gate. Ellie unfastened her headcollar and, feeling a bit guilty about giving up and shouting at her, went to pat her, but Hope simply wheeled away and cantered off, kicking up her heels defiantly.

Ellie heaved a sigh and thought of Spirit nuzzling her and breathing on her hands, pushing his head against her, standing with her for hours. She had such a special bond with Spirit. It would never be the same with Hope. Never. For a moment, she almost wondered about selling the foal on. She stopped her thoughts, shocked at herself, and walked away.

At least Rocky was behaving himself. Stuart had been astonished at the change in him since the time Ellie had spent in his stall. He was like a different horse. He didn't cower in his stable any more and he didn't once try to kick or bite. It was like a switch had been flicked in his brain. Even Ellie found it hard to believe that he could go from fearing people to trusting them so completely, but it seemed that talking to her had been enough.

Still, not wanting to rush him, Ellie decided against trying to back him. She would wait for Joe to come and see if he could help. Instead, she worked Rocky through the maze of poles. He restored her confidence in the training method – and in her own abilities as a trainer. Unlike Hope, he picked up exactly what she meant and in no time at all was responding to the voice commands and signals with the stick, turning corners, backing up, halting, walking over the poles and weaving through them. He seemed to really enjoy it, listening to her intently and trying to please. Feeling good about the progress he was making, Ellie did two sessions with him a day. She didn't try Hope again, though, telling herself that she would wait until the foal was a bit older.

'I can't believe the change in Rocky,' Luke said, coming into the tackroom on Monday morning with

Pip as Ellie was putting the lunge rope away. Ellie looked round in surprise. She'd become used to him going out of his way to avoid talking to her. 'You really have worked a miracle this time.'

The admiration in his eyes was so genuine that Ellie felt her barriers drop slightly. 'Thanks.'

'He's like a different horse.' Luke shot her a teasing look as Pip trotted over to her for some affection. 'That's it, isn't it? I've worked out what you do now. You take a lunatic horse, sell it, buy another that looks just the same and, hey presto, it's suddenly no problem at all and everyone thinks you're some kind of genius.'

Ellie couldn't stop herself. The corners of her mouth curled up as she ruffled the little dog's head. 'Got it in one. You've worked out *exactly* how I do it.'

They smiled and for a moment the tension between them seemed to relax. *I've missed this*, Ellie thought suddenly. *I've missed him.*

Luke gave a sudden sigh. 'It's tough at the moment, isn't it?'

'Yeah,' she admitted. 'Len . . . all the horses . . . so much to do.'

They gave each other a look of shared understanding.

Luke broke the silence. 'That necklace looks good on you.' She realized he was looking at her neck where she wore the necklace he'd given her.

Ellie wore it all the time. 'Thanks.' Their eyes met

and Ellie felt her stomach curl. The moment was broken by Stuart calling her name outside. Ellie stayed where she was, but Luke hastily stepped back. At the same moment his mobile rang. He pulled it out of his pocket and checked the screen, then hit the ANSWER button.

'Hi, Anna.'

Ellie could hear a faint high voice on the other end of the phone. It sounded as if Anna was cross.

'Look, I've told you, I can't come over today,' said Luke, going to the door. 'Joe's coming back and –' He broke off. 'Yeah, of course you're important, babe, but there's a lot of stuff going on here right now. Can't you understand that?' He strode out, phone to his ear, back tense.

Ellie felt like a balloon that had just been pricked. She took a deep breath. *Don't think about him*, she told herself. *He's going out with Anna. Don't think about him at all.* And lifting her chin, she walked out to find Stuart and see what he wanted.

Joe arrived after lunch. Ellie had been looking forward to it so much, and yet when he left the taxi and came up the yard she found herself hanging back awkwardly. It was so strange to see him there, actually there, his face tanned and his sandy-brown hair bleached lighter from the sun, but his familiar grin in place.

'You're back!' Helen cried in delight as he dropped his bags, and she and Sasha greeted him with hugs. Stuart and Luke shook his hand and clapped him on the back.

'Welcome home!' said Luke.

Ellie hovered on the edge of the group, waiting for Joe to turn to her. 'Missed me?' he asked with a grin.

She nodded and the next second he was giving her the biggest bear hug ever.

She gasped in surprise. As she felt him swing her round, her awkwardness melted away and she put her arms round his neck, hugging him back. 'Oh, I have missed you! I have!' she said, her eyes shining as he put her down. 'Oh, Joe!' She hugged him again tightly and heard him laugh.

As they separated, they both beamed at each other.

'Well, ah've sure missed you, honey,' said Joe, putting on a bad Canadian accent.

She laughed again.

'Better get on with stuff,' said Luke, swinging round suddenly. 'Good to have you back, Joe,' he called over his shoulder.

'Really good,' agreed Stuart.

'I'll help you with your bags,' Ellie said happily to Joe. 'Let's dump them inside and then you can see the new horses, Lexi and Rocky.'

'What about the foal? You said you'd bought her.'

'Yeah.'

'Have you been doing loads with her?'

Ellie felt guilty. 'Oh, bits and pieces. It's been really busy round here.'

'Yeah, I bet! So tell me all the news.'

They didn't stop talking all afternoon. After dropping his bags in the house, they walked round the yard, catching up and letting him say hi to all the horses. In next to no time Joe was sweeping up, doing the feeds, filling haynets, chatting to Sasha and Helen. It was as if he'd never been away.

'So you've really met Pat Parelli and Monty Roberts?' said Helen, naming two very well-known horse trainers.

'Yeah, well, I've been to clinics given by both of them.'

'What about film stars?' said Sasha. 'Have you met any of them?'

Joe grinned. 'Nope, I'm afraid not too many of them come to the ranch.'

'What's it like?' asked Ellie.

'Massive. And the mountains . . . you can't describe them. You'd love it,' he said to her. 'It's just empty beautiful countryside for miles and miles. There are wild horses there and everything. And the people are cool.'

'How many grooms are there?'

'We're called stablehands over there and there're ten of us. Ray's a great boss.'

The talking went on and on. Ellie noticed that Luke didn't say much to Joe. She was surprised. He'd seemed happy enough that Joe was coming home. The two of them were so different they were never going to be best friends, but they'd always got on well. But Luke hardly came to chat with Joe at all. The only time she saw him was when he came into the tackroom while she and Joe were putting some headcollars away. She was laughing as Joe described Ray putting him on a horse and making him ride it without a saddle or bridle. 'I'd love to have seen that!' she said.

Luke came in and dumped a grooming kit at her feet. 'You left this in Picasso's stall.'

'Yeah, sorry, I forgot about it when Joe arrived,' said Ellie.

'Well, don't forget about it again!' Luke snapped. 'Picasso could have trodden on it.'

'Who turned you into Len for the day?' Ellie said, surprised and annoyed by his tone.

'I'm just saying.' Luke walked out, his face set.

'Well, don't!' she shouted after him, her anger flaring to meet his.

She saw Joe's startled expression. 'What's up with the pair of you?'

'Nothing.'

'I thought you were getting on better. You seemed to be before I left and you said he was really good when Spirit . . .' He hesitated, not saying the word. 'Well, with Spirit and everything.'

'Yeah, well, I don't know what goes on in his brain!' Ellie said, grimacing. 'Who does? Come on, let's not talk about him. Tell me about the people you work with. Who are your friends?'

'Well, Andy, Brad, Pippa and Lucy are the people I hang round with most. Here, I've got some pictures on my phone . . .' And they were off again, talking non-stop.

Anna Hallett arrived at four o'clock in her sports car, to ride Lucifer and see Luke.

'I told you they'd started going out, didn't I?' Ellie said to Joe in a low voice as Anna walked on to the yard.

Joe nodded as they watched from Starlight's stable. 'So it's all official now.'

'Yeah.'

'They do look good together,' said Joe as Luke went over to greet Anna.

'So should we go for a ride?' Ellie said, changing the subject. 'We could take out Milly and Wisp. They both need exercising.'

'I wish Barney was still here,' Joe said, nodding.

'Yeah.' Ellie squeezed his hand. 'I miss him too. He's gone to a really nice home, though. His new owner adores him.'

Joe nodded. Having been at the stables all his life, he was used to horses and ponies being sold on. 'That's good. And yeah, let's have a ride. I want to go out in the woods.' His phone buzzed with a new text.

He checked it and grinned. 'It's just Lucy wanting to know I've arrived here OK. She's so nice, you'd like her.' He texted back quickly. Ellie watched him. She knew him so well. He must like this girl Lucy to be so rapid in replying.

Joe put his phone in his pocket and they fetched the tack. On the way to the tackroom, they passed Anna and Luke standing by the wash-stall. 'I can't believe you wouldn't come out for lunch,' Anna was saying crossly. 'You said you would last week.'

'Yes, but a lot's happened since then. I thought I'd be able to have the day off, but that was before Len's accident.' Luke sounded annoyed. 'I don't see why you can't understand that.'

Ellie and Joe exchanged looks and went into the tackroom. 'She seems high maintenance,' commented Joe, rolling his eyes.

'Oh, yes,' said Ellie, nodding. 'She is!'

It was brilliant being back in the woods with Joe. They jumped some logs, cantered up and down grassy banks, and then let the ponies walk along the track to cool down. The mud was hard under the ponies' hooves and the sun shone through the green leaves, dappling the ground. The banks at the side of the tracks were covered with a riot of pink and yellow flowers, with bees buzzing in and out of them.

'It's good to be back,' said Joe with a contented sigh. 'Canada's great, but it's good being home too. I must go and see Dad in the morning.'

'Luke says he's in a really bad mood.'

'He's going to hate crutches,' said Joe.

Ellie nodded. She wasn't looking forward to Len coming back. The yard was a much happier place without his constant barking and shouting, cursing and bad temper.

'So, does it seem different being back here?' she said.

'Kind of. I know it sounds weird, but it looks smaller than I'd remembered. I guess most of it is the same, though. Just some stuff has changed.' He gave her a sideways glance. 'It's strange Spirit not being here.'

Ellie looked at Milly's flaxen mane and nodded.

Joe hesitated. 'Do you . . . do you still really miss him?'

Ellie couldn't begin to express the mix of feelings inside. 'Yes,' was all she managed to say. 'Oh, Joe,' she whispered, wishing she could tell him everything.

But he didn't understand the feeling behind her words. How could he? 'It hurts?' he said.

Ellie almost felt like laughing. If it was just the hurt . . . but it wasn't. There was so much more. The conflict – feeling torn between two worlds, wanting desperately to hold on to Spirit, but wanting to spend her time helping troubled horses too. Worrying about Spirit – about him being lonely and missing other horses and about the increasing sense of quietness about him . . .

Maybe there's a reason why the dead don't come back.

No! She slammed Spirit's words away.

It'll be OK, she told herself, refusing to contemplate giving up. *It'll all be fine.*

'Ellie?'

She realized she'd spoken the last thought aloud. 'Sorry,' she said quickly.

'It's OK. You probably don't want to talk about it. I shouldn't have asked.'

'No, it's all right. It would have been strange if you hadn't, but I don't want to talk about it any more.'

Joe's eyes were full of understanding. 'Sure. Come on. They've cooled down now. Let's have another canter.' They picked up their reins and let the ponies canter on through the trees.

Chapter Fifteen

Leading Rocky to the circular ring beside the car park the next morning, Ellie felt excited. Joe was walking beside her, a saddle and bridle slung over his arm. White clouds fluffed out across the pale blue sky.

'You really think I should do it?' Ellie said. She'd seen Joe doing join-up with horses before and putting a saddle and bridle on them for the first time, but she'd never done it herself.

'Definitely. He trusts you. From what you've said, he's had a traumatic time being broken in before. It's better that it's you who works with him now.' Joe's green eyes met hers. 'And I know you can do it.'

Ellie bit back her grin. She had to stay calm. Just like when she was connecting with horses, she needed to be steady, focused.

Once in the ring she unclipped Rocky's leadrope. He gave her an uncertain look and came towards her, nudging her with his nose as if to say *what are you doing?*

'It's OK,' she reassured him. 'Trust me.'

'Send him away!' Joe called from the gate. Ellie lifted her arms. With a snort, but not looking too alarmed, Rocky trotted away to the fence and round the ring.

Ellie knew that she had to send him away from her, chase him on, let him run from her for as long as he wanted and then, when he showed with his body language that he was tired of running and wanted to come and be close and stand still, she had to respond and let him. Swinging the leadrope and using her arms, she drove Rocky on, positioning her body square to his. He plunged into a canter and cantered round the school. Ellie watched him like a hawk. She knew join-up worked, but she also knew Rocky and knew they had a special relationship. If he showed any signs of being scared or seriously stressed by what she was doing, she would stop. But he didn't. He cantered fast, but he didn't look scared.

'Block his movement, send him the other way!' Joe called. Moving quickly so her body was aimed in front of Rocky's head, Ellie lifted her arms. The bay bounced to a stop, wheeled round and cantered in the other direction. Several times, Ellie repeated the action. She knew that this part, the sending away, was vital; it mirrored how mares treated young horses in the herd. Sending them away, waiting for signs of submission, and then letting them close.

Rocky didn't have to canter round long before he was looking to come close to her. First his inside ears seemed to fix on her, then he slowed to a trot, his head reaching down to the ground. Within one more circuit he had started to lick and chew. Ellie knew the signs. They were similar in many ways to the ones a horse gave when healing was working.

'Drop your gaze! Turn away from him!' Joe called.

But Ellie was already doing it. Turning sideways on to the horse, she made her body language as unthreatening as possible, dropping her shoulders, avoiding eye contact. She kept moving on the spot so that her side was always to him. She heard his trot slow to a walk. Hearing him stop and snort, she waited. He only hesitated a second before walking over to her and touching her shoulder with his muzzle.

'That was brilliant,' Joe said as Ellie rubbed Rocky's neck. 'Most horses won't come in at first; you have to send them away again and again. Work your hands over him.'

Ellie stroked Rocky all over, across his back, down his legs, over his face, and then she walked away. With a snort, he followed her, just like a very large dog. Wherever she went, so did he.

Her heart leapt in her chest as she stopped again

and stroked him. He'd joined-up with her. It had been easier than she'd dared to imagine.

'Try sending him away again,' advised Joe.

She did, but within a few circuits Rocky asked to come close, and when she stopped sending him, he trotted in and halted beside her.

'He's a natural at this,' said Joe, smiling. 'You're a real quick learner, aren't you, Rocky? I think he's ready to try some tack,' said Joe as Ellie walked over to the gate with Rocky following.

Given everything Rocky had been through, Ellie was astonished when he let them put on the saddle and bridle without a fuss. He nuzzled her, absolute trust in his eyes. She led him round and then Joe came into the ring and mounted. They had decided it would be best if Ellie could be beside Rocky to soothe and reassure him.

His ears flickered as Joe got on and for a moment he tensed, but as Ellie stroked him and murmured to him, his head lowered and he relaxed. She led Joe round the ring and then he dismounted and legged her up into the saddle. Like any young horse, Rocky was slightly unbalanced by having a rider on his back, but he walked out willingly, halting when she applied the gentlest pressure on his mouth and walking on when she touched him gently with her heels.

'It's amazing!' she said to Joe, beaming from ear

to ear and patting Rocky. 'If you'd seen what he did with Uncle Len, you wouldn't believe it was the same horse.'

'Shows what can be done if you work with the horse,' said Joe. 'And not try and force them.'

They heard the sound of a car's engine coming down the lane. It was Anna Hallett. She drove into the car park and stepped out of the sports car.

'Is that Rocky?' she said, coming to the gate.

Ellie nodded. 'We've just got on him for the first time.' Stuart had decided it would be best not to mention to the Halletts that Rocky was the horse responsible for Len's fall.

'Oh.' Anna turned away. 'Where's Luke?'

Ellie didn't need to answer – having heard the car, Luke appeared. 'Hey,' he said, spotting Ellie on Rocky. 'You're riding him!'

'Yeah, look!' Ellie rode Rocky round the school, halted him and then walked him on again, patting him a lot. He walked with his ears pricked as if wondering what all the fuss was about. Ellie looked at Luke, the atmosphere between them forgotten in her delight. 'Isn't it great?'

'It's amazing!' Luke grinned. 'My theory has to be right. That is no way the same horse.'

They smiled at the shared joke and Ellie felt her heart flip.

'I don't actually see what's *that* amazing,' said

Anna, flicking her ponytail. 'I mean, he's just walking and halting.'

'But if you'd seen what he was like when Len . . . when someone first got on him,' said Luke. 'He was mad. Ellie's done an incredible job.' He smiled at her again.

'Joe as well,' Ellie said, not wanting to take all the credit. 'He helped me do the join-up.'

'It's nothing really to do with me. You did everything with him. I've just been watching. You'll have him trotting tomorrow by the looks of things.'

'Awesome!' said Luke.

'It's not that big a deal!' snapped Anna

Luke turned to her. 'It *is* that big a deal. Surely even you can see that?'

What do you mean, even *I* can see that?'

'What I said!'

Anna glared at him and marched away up the yard.

'Oh, for heaven's sake.' Luke groaned and rolled his eyes, then went after her.

Joe chuckled. 'Look's as if Luke's got his hands full.'

Ellie nodded and tried not to think about it. She dismounted. 'Rocky's done enough for today. Let's take him in.'

In the afternoon, Joe and Luke went to see Len. In the evening, just Ellie and Joe were in the house. Luke had gone off to meet Anna, although Ellie had picked up a feeling he wasn't that happy about it. Still, she was glad. It was lovely being on her own with Joe.

'So what did you think when you saw your dad?' she asked as they ate jacket potatoes loaded with butter and cheese in front of the TV.

'Well, Luke was right. He's in a foul mood. He's going to be unbearable when he comes home.'

'When will that be?' Ellie wished she could feel happier at the thought of her uncle leaving hospital, but it was hard.

'Tomorrow, I think. So how's he been generally? I mean, before the accident?'

'Worse than ever,' replied Ellie. 'He was OK at Hickstead, but the rest of the time . . .' She shook her head. 'I don't know, it's as if the horses are machines to him now.' She looked at Joe to see if he understood. 'He just calls them "it" or "that bay", or sometimes even "that animal".'

'I know. He was becoming more like that before I left,' Joe admitted. 'I suppose I didn't really notice it until I went to Canada and stayed with Ray. He's so not like that. He strokes all the horses, calls them by name, spends time with them. He still seems to like riding as well. Whereas Dad . . . yeah, you're right, it's as if they're machines. He didn't used to be like this.' He sighed. 'I wish I could get him to change.'

He looked so downcast that Ellie changed the

subject. 'Come on, tell me more about Canada and your friends there.' She took a mouthful of jacket potato. 'Lucy seems to text you quite a lot.' She shot him a sideways look. From the photos she'd seen on his phone, Lucy looked pretty. She had lots of curly hair and green eyes, very like Joe's.

'Oh, Lucy's just Lucy.' Joe shrugged, but Ellie saw the faint telltale blush on his cheekbones and noticed how he was avoiding her gaze.

'Are you going out with her?' she asked directly.

'No . . .' There was a slight hesitation in his voice.

'Not yet?' prompted Ellie, filling in the gaps.

'Not yet,' admitted Joe.

Ellie paused, wondering how she felt about Joe going out with someone else, but she was relieved that she didn't really mind. She'd mind if Joe went out with someone not nice, someone who didn't treat him well, but that was it. He was her friend now, nothing more. Joe ran a hand through his hair. 'I dunno. She might not like me anyway – not in that way.'

'I'd say, judging by the number of texts she sends, she does,' said Ellie wryly.

Joe looked at her. 'Do you mind?'

'No,' she said honestly, hearing the worry in his voice. 'So what's she like?'

'Nice. Like you in a way, but not as mad.'

'So boring then?' Ellie raised her eyebrows teasingly.

'Not boring. Just a bit . . . a bit safer.' He rushed

on, seeing her expression. 'I love you, Els. You know that, but even if we weren't cousins, it would never have worked. You're amazing – the coolest person I know – you're so unstoppable, but I can't be like that. We wouldn't be right for each other. You need someone who's more like you – someone else.'

A picture of Luke came into Ellie's head. She pushed it crossly away. 'I wish people would stop telling me I need someone else,' she muttered.

Joe looked puzzled. 'What?'

Ellie shook her head. 'It doesn't matter,' she sighed.

'No, what did you mean?'

'I don't want to talk about it.'

Joe nodded. 'Sure.' He turned back to his jacket potato.

She inwardly shook her head. It was so Joe. He'd never push anything, he'd always back off. He was right. They were the best of friends, but they would never have been right for each other. 'So,' she said, forcing lightness into her voice as she added more butter to her potato, 'tell me more about Lucy. How old is she? Why else do you like her so much?'

Joe smiled and began to talk.

They didn't stay up late that night. Ellie had just gone to bed when she heard Luke return unusually early. He wasn't in the best of the moods by the sound of it. He slammed the back door and then his bedroom door.

Maybe his date with Anna hadn't gone that well then. Trying not to feel too pleased at the thought, Ellie rolled over and shut her eyes.

Luke was still in a bad mood the next morning. Ellie went down to the kitchen to find him banging a carton of milk down on the side because the tab on the foil top under the cap had broken off, leaving him unable to pour the milk.

'What's the matter with you?' Ellie asked, fetching some scissors and cutting open the foil as he leant back against the sink, arms folded across his chest.

Luke took a breath and for a moment she thought he would tell her, but then he shook his head and walked out of the kitchen.

'Do you want a coffee?' she called, seeing the mug on the side with coffee granules in it.

He didn't answer as the back door slammed behind him.

'Temper, temper,' Ellie muttered, but she felt surprised. Luke was hardly ever in a bad mood.

Later that morning she found out why. Grooming Rocky, she heard Helen go into the stall next door, where Sasha was brushing Lexi over. 'Have you heard the latest?' Helen said.

'What?'

'Luke and Miss I've-Got-A-Rich-Daddy have split up.'

Ellie paused in her grooming.

'She dumped him!' Sasha's voice was incredulous.

'No, *he* dumped her.'

'Why?'

'Her personality bypass maybe?' Helen chuckled.

Ellie realized that she had paused with the body brush in mid-air. So Luke and Anna had split up! She cursed herself as she felt her hopes leap. He wasn't interested in her. She knew that.

'Hang on, if Luke dumped her, why's he in such a bad mood this morning?' said Sasha, repeating exactly Ellie's next thought.

'Who knows? Maybe he doesn't have a replacement or three lined up yet. He might have a day or two without a girlfriend.'

Both grooms giggled.

Ellie carried on grooming, but inside her heart was jumping up and down. Determined to ignore it, she swept the brush over Rocky's coat with such force that he turned and gave her a very puzzled look.

Luke seemed just as determined as ever to avoid Ellie that day and for once she had absolutely no idea what was going on his head, but at least she had Joe to hang round with. Together, they rode the horses, groomed and cleaned tack, and then she showed him the progress – or lack of it – that she was making with Hope. He watched as the foal jumped around her in the school, barging her, ignoring the stick, butting Ellie in the back and almost making her fall over.

'I can't do anything with her!' Ellie said in frustration.

'Keep trying,' Joe encouraged.

But Ellie had had enough. 'I think she's just too young for this.'

'She's not. You can work foals younger than her through a grid like that.'

'So you do it!'

'No, it's you she has to work with, Els.'

'Well, what am I doing wrong?' Ellie appealed to him.

'I'm not quite sure.' Joe frowned. 'Look, let's give it a break for now. There's no point going on if you're getting cross. That won't achieve anything. I'll think about it and we can try again in the next few days.'

Ellie sighed and took Hope in. That afternoon, Joe and Luke went to bring Len home. Ellie hesitated over what to do. The important jobs were all finished. Maybe she should bring Hope out and work some more with her . . .

No. She shrank from the thought. Hope would just play her up again. But there were plenty of other things she could do. Maybe she could talk to Lexi and see how the mare was feeling now. Or talk to Rocky about whether being ridden was OK. Also, she'd heard Stuart mention to Helen that Hereward was looking stiff on his left side; maybe she should talk to the big hunter and see if he had injured himself in any way. She shut her eyes. There were so many things that she could be doing. But Spirit . . . She felt the familiar tug at her heart and gave into it. He needed her and she wanted to be with him.

Reaching his grave, she sat down and called to him. She felt his presence, the touch of his invisible muzzle, the brush of his long mane, and felt the peace and happiness that always came over her when she was with him. How could she ever give up this feeling? But then how could she go on living with one foot in one world and one in another?

Letting her hands play in his mane, she felt his yearning – his loneliness too. *Oh, Spirit*, she thought unhappily.

Yes?

She hesitated. What could she say? Should she ask him if he thought it was time for him to leave?

No! She sighed and shook her head. 'It doesn't matter,' she said softly.

Splaying her fingers, she felt his warm breath on them as he sighed deeply. She didn't say anything more and neither did he.

Joe and Luke returned with Len just before feedtime. Ellie went down to meet them. She was shocked by the sight of her uncle. After his enforced bed rest, his face looked pale and he seemed to have lost weight.

Joe took his crutches and helped him out of the car on to them, but when he tried to help him further Len shook him off. 'I can manage. I don't need you fussing round me like a flamin' nursemaid.' He caught sight of Ellie watching. 'And what are you staring at?'

'Nothing,' she said quickly.

'Good.'

Pip went over to investigate and Len hit out angrily at her with a crutch. The dog jumped back. With difficulty, Len started using the crutches to walk up to the yard, but the slope was steep and he struggled. Joe went to help. 'I don't need any bloody help!' Len snarled.

Ellie saw Joe fall back.

'Come on, Len,' said Luke. 'You've fractured your leg. Of course you need a bit of help.'

'When I need help, I'll ask.'

Ellie followed her uncle with Luke and Joe as he made painfully slow progress up the yard.

'What are you three doing following me?' Len demanded. 'It's almost five o'clock. Get up there and help with the feeds.'

'OK,' said Joe, exchanging looks with Ellie. Her heart was sinking. She'd known it would be difficult having Len back on the yard, but he was worse than she'd even imagined he'd be.

Things didn't improve. Determined to re-establish his self-respect when he reached the yard, Len immediately started to find fault.

'Those flower baskets haven't been watered enough. Look at them. And look at the state of the yard.' Ellie looked – there were about three pieces of straw on it. 'It's covered with straw. Fetch a broom, Joe, and start brushing. You can help too,' he grunted to Ellie. 'And, Luke, straighten those headcollars. Stu!'

Stuart came out of the feedroom. 'Hey, Len.'

'Get those bleeding flower baskets watered.'

'Sure thing, boss.'

Ellie fetched a broom and started sweeping with a sigh. Oh yes, her uncle was most definitely home.

Chapter Sixteen

'You're not calling that a groomed horse!' Len snapped to Ellie the next morning as she finished grooming Gem on the yard. Len heaved himself over on his crutches. Gem jumped back in alarm, eyeing the strange sticks Len was leaning on. 'There's mud on his hocks and muck on his neck. Get him done properly.' Len had been back on the yard for a day and a bit now, yet his mood hadn't improved at all. If anything it had grown blacker with the constant frustration at not being able to move around and do the things he usually did. He simply wouldn't stay inside and rest, but hauled himself around, swearing as he tried to get up and down the sloping yard.

There was a show on that day and Luke, Stu and Helen had thankfully escaped to take the liveries there, leaving Joe and Ellie to bear the brunt of Len's anger – it was Sasha's day off so there were just the two of them.

Picking up a brush again, Ellie started to re-groom

Gem, although the patches of mud that Len had supposedly spotted were almost non-existent.

Len went to Troy's stable and tried to get in, but the bolt was stiff and as he tried to pull it across, his crutches slipped.

Ellie hesitated. Whenever people offered help, he bit their heads off.

He looked round over his shoulder. 'Well, don't just stand there gawping at me like I'm some animal in the zoo. Come and help me.'

It seemed that nothing she or anyone else could do would ever be right.

Ellie went over and opened the stable door. Len heaved himself inside and looked Troy up and down assessingly, checking his condition. The friendly hunter came over and reached out to nuzzle him.

'Get off!' Len growled.

Ellie remembered her conversation with Joe and how he'd talked about Ray stroking his horses and enjoying being with them. If only Len could be like that.

When Len had inspected the horses, he had Ellie and Joe up in the ring, riding on Milly and Wisp. Ellie didn't think she'd ever been shouted at more in her life. Nothing she did was right, her hands were too low, her legs too far forward, her back not straight. Every second he wasn't shouting at Joe, he was shouting at her.

'Will you get that ruddy mare going forward!' he yelled for the umpteenth time.

Ellie had to bite her tongue to stop herself from screaming back at him. *She's not a ruddy mare – she's got a name. She's called Milly and she* is *going forward!*

Feeling Ellie's gathering tension, Milly started to mess around, pulling and going sideways, which made Len yell even more. Then he turned on Joe.

'Don't know what Ray's been teaching you, but get your legs on and get that pony on the bit!'

Ellie and Joe were very relieved when they could come in, but they had no break. Len wanted them straight back out on Picasso and Gabriel. And so the day went on until, after lunch, Len announced he needed a rest and they could carry on with working the youngsters.

'I don't think I can stand this,' Ellie muttered.

'Don't think we have a choice,' said Joe.

'Is he going to be like this every single day?'

'I guess so.'

'It's all right for you – you'll be going back to Canada next week.'

'Fancy coming?'

'Yes please!' she begged.

Joe put his arm round her shoulders and gave her a quick hug. 'Come on, let's start working on the youngsters while we don't have Dad bellowing in our ears. Who shall we start with?'

‘How about Sandy? She bucked me off twice when we started backing her a few weeks ago. She’s been all right since, but I have a feeling it’s more because she’s given up fighting rather than that she wants to please. We could try joining-up with her.’

‘Definitely,’ said Joe.

They brought the filly out of the barn and took her down to the circular ring. Ellie caught sight of Len watching them from the kitchen window. Her heart sank. She hoped he wouldn’t come out.

Once they reached the ring, Joe set the mare loose. Ellie settled back to watch. Sandy took longer to join-up than Rocky had, but then she didn’t know Joe. Still, he didn’t give up and soon she was following him around the school.

‘You’ll be taking her in bloody Crufts next!’ Hearing her uncle’s voice, Ellie looked round and realized he’d been watching Joe join-up as he’d made his slow way down from the house to the ring on his crutches. ‘What the hell are you doing, Joe?’

Ellie saw Joe sigh, but he tried to be patient. ‘It’s join-up, Dad. You know what that is. We do lots of it at Ray’s yard. It’s how he starts all his youngsters before he backs them.’

‘That pony’s been backed. You could get on and ride her, no problem.’

‘Yes, but does she trust you?’ said Joe in a level voice. ‘Does she see you as a partner?’

Ellie felt a start of surprise. She was used to Joe backing down when Len challenged him. But the time away had changed him, made him stronger, she realized.

'Partner?' Len rolled his eyes. 'She's the horse. I'm the rider. She'll do what I say.'

'But will she give her heart for you when the chips are down?' Joe persisted. 'Jump that difficult jump when you need her to. Find the stride when you've missed it. That's what a horse who sees you as a partner does.'

Len just snorted derisively. 'Stuff 'n' airy-fairy nonsense if you ask me.'

'It's not nonsense! Joe's talking complete sense!' Ellie's voice rose angrily. 'Why won't you listen to him? Why won't you take any notice?'

'I'll take notice when I see a horse that hasn't already been backed and ridden out for two weeks.' Len pointed at Sandy. 'What does that prove? We've sorted her out already.'

Ellie glared at him. 'You want proof. OK, I'll show you proof.'

'Ellie!' Joe protested.

But the only thing Ellie could think about was proving her uncle wrong. 'Wait here. I'll be back in a minute! Joe, put Sandy away.'

'But . . .'

Ellie was already running up the yard.

*

'What the bleedin' hell . . . ?'

Ellie led Rocky down to the school with his tack on.

Her uncle started shaking his head. 'All right, enough's enough. That horse isn't right in the head. No one's getting on him.'

'It's too late,' Ellie said softly.

Clicking her tongue, she led Rocky into the ring.

'It's OK, Dad,' Joe reassured him. 'It'll be fine. Ellie's been working with him.'

'Come on in,' said Ellie, holding the gate open for Len.

Her uncle hesitated. 'Scared?' she challenged him.

His expression darkened and he pulled himself into the ring on his crutches. Joe shut the gate behind him.

Ellie stroked Rocky's neck and then swung herself easily into the saddle. She heard her uncle's exclamation of alarm. But Rocky stood calmly just as she had known he would. She'd been working with him and riding him every day since she had joined-up with him. She touched her heels to his side and he walked on. She halted, turned, trotted and then brought him to where her uncle was standing.

Her uncle stood staring at her and the horse. Ellie felt overwhelmed with satisfaction. 'See,' she said, dismounting.

With a shake of his head, her uncle turned and made for the gate. Ellie felt a rush of disappointment. Even after seeing Rocky, her uncle still couldn't open his mind enough to accept that the things Joe did worked.

'Open the gate!' Len ordered Joe. 'I won't waste any more time watching this.'

'Dad!' Joe glanced at Ellie's disappointed face and then seemed to make a decision. He shook his head. 'No.'

'Open the ruddy gate,' snapped Len.

'No,' Joe repeated. 'Not until you open your eyes. You can see what Ellie's done, what I've done. You've heard Ray tell you about it. Face it, Dad. This way of training works.'

'I won't be told what to do by you!' Len snarled. 'Now open the gate and get that horse in.'

Father and son glared at each other.

Ellie expected Joe to back down, but he didn't. Only once had she ever seen him stand up to his dad like this before – straight after Len had had his pony, Merlin, put to sleep.

'No,' Joe said, shaking his head. '*You* get Rocky in. Ellie, untack him.'

She frowned. 'What?'

She wasn't the only one. 'I can't get a bloody horse in. Look at me!' Len nodded furiously at his crutches. 'I can't even open the bloody gate.'

'I'll open the gate once you catch Rocky. Ellie, take his tack off,' Joe repeated, climbing out of the ring.

Ellie suddenly thought she knew what Joe was trying to do. Would it work? While her uncle swore at Joe and cursed, turning the air blue with his language, she unbuckled the girth, slid the saddle off, and then undid the bridle and took it off too. Rocky looked at her in surprise. She patted his neck and raised her arms, sending him away. Used to join-up now, he seemed to accept that was what she wanted him to do and he trotted away to the side of the ring happily.

She went to the side and ducked out between the bars of the fence with the tack.

Suddenly her uncle realized he was in there alone. 'What the hell are you two playing at?' He glanced at Rocky, who had slowed to a walk, and then looked at Ellie and Joe outside the gate. 'I'll murder you when I get out of here, Joe, you just see if I don't!'

Joe looked at him levelly. 'You won't be getting out until you catch Rocky.'

'I can't catch that flamin' horse!'

'You can. You've seen me do join-up. Now you do it – get him to come to you. Otherwise you'll be in there for a long time.' Joe checked his watch. 'Stu and Luke won't be back for about another five hours, I reckon.' He started to back away from the gate.

'Don't you dare go, Joe!' Len roared, making Rocky jump into a trot again.

'Sorry, Dad, but I think you've lost track of why you started working with horses in the first place and you need to be reminded. Horses are amazing. They've got thoughts, feelings, emotions, and you get so much more out of it if you work with them rather than forcing them. It's time you learnt that and I reckon this is the only way.'

Joe backed up further. Ellie went with him. 'Are you sure about this?' she whispered uncertainly.

Joe nodded and she saw a sudden steeliness in his gaze that she had never seen before. 'He's got to realize.'

Len swore loudly and then tried to haul himself towards Rocky. For a moment the horse stood still, but then he took off as Len swore again. He cantered around the ring. 'Come here, you daft bugger!' shouted Len, swinging a crutch at him, but that just made Rocky canter faster.

Ellie could see the frustration and fury on Len's face, the total feeling of impotence raging through him at his loss of control.

'I said come here!' he yelled, losing his temper with Joe, with the horse. 'Stupid, flamin' . . .' He ranted and raved, swinging his crutch, anger spilling out of him. Stumbling again towards the horse, Len caught himself on his crutches and swore violently as Rocky cantered on. 'Bloody useless legs. . .' His voice broke up with a sob. Ellie saw his shoulders shake and shot an alarmed look at Joe. With another sob, the fight suddenly seem to evaporate from Len. He slumped over his crutches as he gave in to the frustration, accepting his physical restraint.

'Joe, we should go to him,' said Ellie anxiously.

'Wait. Look what's happening.' Joe nodded to where Rocky had slowed to a halt. He was staring at Len's bowed, shaking shoulders with a slightly uncertain expression. He wavered and then with a snort he cautiously approached, just as if it was a normal join-up.

Ellie caught her breath. Reaching Len's back, Rocky stretched out his muzzle. Len slowly looked round. Ellie saw the incredulity on his face. His shoulders stopped shaking and, leaning on his elbow on the crutch, he simply stared at the horse and the horse stared back. Rocky waited for Len to move towards him and pat him. When the man didn't, Rocky stepped closer and touched Len's hand with his muzzle.

Len reached up with his hand. Rocky blew on his fingers and then lifted his nose and breathed on Len's face.

Ellie watched spellbound as tears glittered suddenly in Len's eyes. He touched the horse's neck and then his face. The horse looked at him trustingly and didn't move. Ellie felt tears spring to her own eyes. Rocky, once so damaged and in need of healing, was now doing the healing himself simply by being a horse. She shook her head. Horses – they were so strong and powerful, yet so eager to trust and love despite what humans often did to them.

Ellie saw Len's lips start to move as he talked to the horse, caressing him all the time with his hand. She realized she'd never seen him stroke a horse before apart from as a fleeting reward when one performed well.

'It's worked,' she whispered.

Joe's eyes were fixed on his dad and Rocky. Slowly, Len adjusted himself on his crutches and began to make his way painfully to the gate.

Rocky followed at his shoulder. Len glanced round and a smile crossed his face, a genuine smile, so rare it was like a glimpse of sun on a winter's day.

Joe went down to the gate to meet him, with Ellie following. When they reached the gate, Joe unfastened it. For a moment, he and Len just stared at each other.

'I'm sorry, but you needed to be reminded, Dad,' Joe said quietly.

Len nodded slowly. 'Aye.' He touched Rocky's neck. 'You're right, lad. I did.'

Chapter Seventeen

'What have you done to Len?' Luke demanded as he cornered Ellie and Joe in the feedroom later that day. 'How did you do it? He's not been like this for years.'

He and Stuart had arrived back from the show to find Len doing a final check after feedtime. But he wasn't just glancing briefly into each stall as he usually did; he was stopping at each door, talking to the horses who came to greet him, simply watching the others as they pulled at their haynets or nosed their beds. For the first time since Ellie had known him, he seemed to simply take pleasure in being around the horses.

Luke looked at Ellie. 'Was this you again? Is it something you've done?'

'No, not me. It was Joe,' said Ellie. 'He made Len do join-up with Rocky and since then he's been different.'

'Seriously?'

Joe nodded.

'But how the hell did you make him do a join-up?'

Joe looked uncomfortable. 'Not exactly willingly,' he admitted, and told Luke what had happened.

Luke's eyes widened. 'You shut Len in the ring and wouldn't let him out.' He laughed incredulously. 'Respect, Joe! Even I wouldn't do that – I don't think even *Ellie* would.'

Their eyes met for a second. She looked quickly away. Joe was continuing.

'I think it made Dad remember why he wanted to work with horses in the first place. He's been so much better to be around this afternoon. He's not shouted anything like as much.'

'So do you reckon he'll seriously start using join-up and things like that?' Luke asked.

Joe shrugged. 'You know Dad, I don't think he'll change completely, but he says he'll try using join-up, and if he starts with that . . . well, who knows, maybe he'll move into the whole natural horsemanship thing and really start to change how he does stuff.'

'I hope so,' said Ellie. It was so nice to see her uncle talking to the horses and stroking them, but even better to see him treating Joe with a new respect. As she and Joe had cleaned tack that afternoon, Len had come in to talk with them, asking Joe about everything he'd learnt, and he'd seemed to really listen to the answers, taking it all in. Ellie prayed it was the start of a new and more equal relationship between them. She just wished Joe didn't have to go back to Canada so soon.

But he did. His return plane ticket was booked for a few days' time and she could tell, deep down, he was looking forward to returning. As she watched him pack on the day he was leaving, she was vividly reminded of the first time he'd left and of how things had changed since. Back then, Joe would never have stood up to Len – he'd never have had the courage to make him join-up with Rocky – but staying with Ray and being encouraged by him had given Joe a new confidence. Never in a million years would Ellie have thought she'd be glad Joe had been sent to Canada, but now she felt happy about it and was glad for him that he was going back, even though she would really miss him. But Joe would be back with Ray – back to the yard where he could practise natural horsemanship techniques to his heart's content – and back to Lucy . . .

She picked up a sock. 'Here. Don't forget this.'

He looked at her. 'Don't you want to keep it to remember me by?' he teased.

'Gross! Like I'd want one of your smelly socks!' She chucked it at him.

Joe grinned, catching it and shoving it in his rucksack. 'It's strange to be leaving. Saying goodbye all over again.' His expression grew more serious.

'It's hard. I want to be here – particularly with the way Dad's been behaving the last few days. But I also want to be back there.' He looked rueful. 'I wish people could be in two places at once.'

Ellie sighed, thinking how often she'd been wishing the same thing recently. But seeing the sadness on Joe's face, she forced herself to be positive. 'You'll have a great time when you're there. You know you will. It's just the goodbye bit that's tough.'

Joe nodded. 'Last time I went, I kept thinking about a saying of your mum's you'd told me about. That one about endings?'

'Every ending's a new beginning?' Ellie said.

'Yeah. It helped. I tried to make myself see going to Canada like that. It *is* hard to say goodbye to one life and start another, but it's the right thing to do because if you don't do it, you just stay in the same place – stuck, nothing ever changing.' Joe ran a hand through his hair. 'Saying goodbye to what you know *is* a scary thing to do, though.'

Ellie didn't speak.

Joe gave her a sympathetic look. 'But you know that. It must have been the same for you when you left New Zealand.'

Ellie wasn't thinking about New Zealand. It was Spirit who was in her mind. She let her thoughts take her where she didn't want to go. Should she be saying goodbye to him? Was that the right thing to do? Her heart twisted savagely. No. How could it be? How could saying goodbye to Spirit ever be right?

Unless he was lonely, yearning to go, staying only for her – unless she really was torn in two, unable to be with him and also give the other horses the time that they needed . . .

She felt as if she was being pulled inexorably in one direction while she fought and fought to stay where she was. She pushed the thoughts away. She didn't want to hear them.

'I've been thinking about Hope,' Joe went on. 'I know we've had no time to do anything with her the last few days, but do you want to bring her out now? I've got a little while before Stu takes me to the airport.'

'Yeah. Sure,' said Ellie, eager for the distraction.

Joe threw the last few things into his rucksack and they went outside. It was a sunny afternoon, just a slight breeze streaking the white clouds across the blue sky. Joe went to lay some poles out in a grid in the school, while Ellie fetched Hope from the field. Hope, however, had other ideas. She trotted away whenever Ellie came close.

'Oh, come on, Hope!' Ellie groaned, walking after her, but the foal wheeled away. 'Stop being so annoying!' Ellie exclaimed.

The foal hid behind Gem. She looked cute, but all Ellie felt was a rush of exasperation.

'Come here!'

Hope turned her back, and as soon as Ellie walked round Gem, she cantered off again.

With a sigh of frustration, Ellie went back to the stable and fetched some foal nuts in a bucket. As she shook them, the foal came eagerly. She plunged her head into the bucket and Ellie slipped her headcollar on.

'Right, let's take you up to the ring and get this over and done with. Then you can come back out and I can catch up with other things.'

The foal nipped her.

'Stop it!' Ellie said crossly, pushing her away.

Hope nipped her again. 'No!' Ellie spoke even more sharply.

Hope jogged and pulled beside her as Ellie led her out of the field and up to the school.

Joe had the training stick and lunge line ready. 'OK, let's see you try to walk and halt her, and then we'll move on to backing up.'

Ellie remembered what she'd been doing with Rocky and tried to teach the foal to move forward at a signal from her voice and from the lunge rein, but Hope just seemed determined not to cooperate. When Ellie asked her to move forward, she planted her feet or swung round. When Ellie did get her moving and asked her to stop, she went faster. Ellie grew more and more frustrated and when she glanced at Joe she saw a frown deepening on his face.

'Oh, for goodness' sake!' she burst out as Hope trod on her foot when she was trying to get her to halt. 'This is pointless, Joe! She won't do anything I say.'

'OK, stop. Let me try with her and see how she is with me,' said Joe.

He and Ellie swapped places. Ellie watched as Joe started working with the filly in his quiet, patient way, correcting her gently, guiding her, praising her when she was good. Hope kept glancing round to where Ellie was standing, but she soon started to walk and halt and back up on command.

Ellie felt increasingly depressed. In ten minutes Joe had achieved more than she had in several sessions.

Joe halted Hope. 'OK, you come and have a try now.'

'What's the point?' Ellie muttered. 'She just won't do it for me.'

'Well, she won't if you have that attitude!' said Joe.

Ellie looked up at the unusual sharpness in his tone.

'Ellie, you can't work a horse if you start off by thinking you'll fail,' he said. 'You know that.' He shook his head. 'This is so not like you. You're the most positive person I know normally. Why are you giving up so easily with Hope?'

Ellie swallowed. 'I don't think she likes me.'

'Doesn't like you?' Joe stared. 'Don't be daft, Els! Of course she does. All the time I've been working her she's been looking over at you. All the nipping and messing around she does, it's just to get *your* attention. Surely you can see that?'

'But she's got my attention when I'm working her, so why do it?' Ellie protested.

'She's got your attention, but you're not engaging with her.' Comprehension suddenly dawned on Joe's face. 'Of course! I've been trying to figure out what's wrong between the two of you and that's it – you're not connecting with her. I've never seen you like that with a horse before. Usually whatever you're doing – whether you're riding, working a horse in hand, even just grooming – you do it wholeheartedly and you engage completely with the horse you're working with. But not with Hope. I can see it in your eyes. I can feel it when you're working with her and I think she can feel it too. That's why she's messing around, Ellie, I think she likes you, but she doesn't think you like her.'

'But that's crazy!' Ellie protested. 'Of course I like her. I like all horses!' She shook her head. Joe didn't know what he was talking about. She *had* connected with the foal – when Hope had been really ill she'd spoken to her, talked to her, made her better . . .

But even as she denied it in her head, a little part of her was curling up, squirming as she recognized the truth in Joe's words.

He *was* right. She had connected with Hope then, but almost from the moment she'd bought her she had stopped engaging with her. No wonder the little filly had been confused and started playing up. Ellie hadn't once tried to talk to her properly. She hadn't spent time in the stable with her. If anything she'd avoided her.

She stared at Joe. 'Oh God!' she groaned. 'You're right.'

Joe led Hope over. 'Is it because of Spirit? Maybe . . .' He hesitated. 'Maybe you don't want to love another horse – you're scared?'

'No.' Ellie spoke honestly. She knew it wasn't that. She was no coward when it came to love. But she also knew it *was* because of Spirit. Looking at Hope, she finally realized what she'd been doing. A bit of her felt that if she loved the little filly, if she gave her heart to her properly, it would somehow be an acceptance that Spirit had really gone from her life – her life here on the yard. She didn't want to think that, she wanted to believe things could be as they were before. To stop it being true, she'd avoided the little filly, not allowing herself to love her, refusing to admit that things had changed and Spirit would never properly come back.

The foal pulled towards her, soft lips catching at Ellie's fingers, her eyes dark and hopeful as she sought attention.

'You're really telling me she doesn't like you?' Joe said softly.

Ellie breathed in Hope's warm, sweet, living smell and felt tears catch in her throat. What had she been doing? Hope was just a baby. She didn't understand. Ellie remembered the promise she'd made that she would always look after her. That meant more than just grooming and feeding; it meant loving her too.

Joe checked his watch. 'I'd better put my stuff together. But please don't give up with Hope.' He ruffled the foal's mane. 'She's brilliant, so like you – feisty, stubborn, a bit nutty too. I think you could have an amazing partnership with her if you wanted it.' His eyes met hers. 'I know she'll never be Spirit, but she does love you, Els. Give her a chance. Love her back.'

Handing the leadrope to her, he swung himself over the gate.

Ellie led Hope down to her stable. She felt numb on the outside, but inside her thoughts were whirling. As she took off Hope's headcollar, the foal gave her a hard shove with her nose. Instead of telling her off or walking away as she usually would have done, Ellie placed a hand on either side of the foal's head and gently stroked with her thumbs. At first Hope tensed, but then gradually she relaxed and her head sank down, her muzzle coming to rest against Ellie's chest. Ellie swallowed. She'd been trying to kid herself, tell herself that nothing had changed. But it had. Spirit was a ghost. Her real life wasn't with him like she felt it was, it was here, and the time she spent with him would always be stolen time. Something slipped into place in her brain with a silent click. Suddenly she knew that no matter how much she wanted to fight it, she couldn't. Whether she liked it or not, things had changed.

She swallowed, realizing what she had to do. Hard as it was, impossible as it seemed, she and Spirit had to say goodbye. He'd lived with her, come back from the grave for her, but their time together had come to an end.

Tears swelled in her throat. Sensing her distress, Hope pushed closer. Ellie kissed her forehead, fighting back the tears.

The living need you.

Spirit's words echoed in her mind. Yes, Hope needed her; the other horses needed her. She desperately needed Spirit, but she had to be brave.

'I will make you happy,' she promised Hope, her heart aching. 'I will love you.'

Leaving the stable, Ellie rested for a moment against the door, her back pressing into the hard wood. How could she do this? Her mind spun down into a black void. She felt so happy when she was with Spirit. How could she possibly find the courage to let him go? She started to shake, involuntary tremors running through her. She would be able to do so much good, help so many horses, but she'd be so lonely.

'Ellie!' she heard Joe's shout on the main yard.

Hold it together, she told herself. *Just for a while.*

Swallowing, she took a breath and walked on to the yard. By the time she reached the others, the shaking had stopped. Stuart was waiting with the car keys in his hands while Joe said goodbye to everyone: Luke, Sasha, Helen, his dad . . .

'You will try join-up again when you're better, won't you, Dad?' Joe said.

Len nodded. 'I'll be bloody better at it than you by the time you get home next!'

Joe smiled at his competitiveness.

'And I want to hear about everything else you're doing over there,' Len went on. 'I'm expecting phone calls this time – and emails.'

'Sure,' said Joe, and Ellie saw the happiness in his eyes. 'See you.' He turned to Ellie. 'Bye, Els.' He stepped forward and hugged her. Shutting her eyes, she felt his arms close round her. She wanted the world to stop, to freeze. If they just stayed where they were everything would be all right . . .

But life never stops. After a few moments, she

felt his grip slacken and he started to pull back. Taking a deep breath, she let him go, fighting back the tears.

Luke looked at her. She didn't meet his eyes, but she sensed his glance and knew he was wondering at the misery on her face. She didn't have the strength to hide it. She managed to control the tears as Joe climbed into the car, but the second Stuart drove off she turned and ran, heading back to Hope's stable. She wanted to be by herself so she could cry and cry.

'Ellie!' As she reached the stable door, she heard Luke following her.

Not now. Go away, she thought, not turning. Her fingers reached for the bolt.

His long strides covered the ground. 'Ellie? Are you all right?'

Shutting her eyes, Ellie swallowed.

The next second she felt his arms round her, pulling her towards him.

'What is it?' he said as, unable to stop herself, she started to cry. He stroked her hair over and over again as if calming a horse. 'Are you really so upset about Joe going? Is there something between you then?'

'No!' The shock stopped her tears for a moment. 'Of course not.'

Was it her imagination or did a look of relief pass through his eyes?

'I'm glad he's gone back – for him. He's happy in Canada,' she went on.

'So why are you so upset? What's happened?' She saw the concern etched on Luke's face. His tone altered suddenly. 'Has someone hurt you?'

'No.' She shook her head. There was no explanation she could give for her tears. 'It's just something, Luke. You can't understand. No one can.' She tried to turn away but then started to sob, leaning instead against his strong chest. Luke held her close, stroking her hair again.

'Oh, Ellie!'

Hearing the groan in his voice, she looked up. He was shaking his head. 'I just can't do this any more,' he said despairingly.

'Do what?' She was taken aback by the look of confusion in his eyes.

His hands gripped her arms. 'Avoid you. Try and stay away from you. Try and behave well for once in my life.'

'Is that what you've been doing?'

'Of course it is!' he burst out. 'Ever since that moment in the horsebox . . . no, for longer than that. I don't know when it started. Maybe when you first walked on the yard. Whenever, why ever, all I know is I've never wanted to be serious about anyone in my life, but I want to be serious about you. I don't know what you've done to me, but I can't see you cry like this and not want to hold you and make you feel better. I can't watch you day after day and not want to kiss you.'

'But I . . . I thought I was just some little kid to you?' she whispered, her mouth suddenly dry.

'Some little kid who I can't stop thinking about, who I want to be with, kiss, talk to . . .' Luke's lips lifted at the corners. 'Be told off by.' He shook his head. 'I know I should stay away. I know I'm too old for you. I know –'

She didn't want to hear any more. She stood on tiptoes and silenced him with a kiss.

Slowly, she sank back and they stared at each other.

He broke the silence, his voice husky, incredulous. 'You feel the same?'

'Of course I do, idiot,' she said softly. 'Surely you know that?'

His hands gripped her more tightly. 'I'll change. I want to be good enough for you. I *will* be good enough.'

She couldn't tear her eyes away from his. 'You already are.'

Luke's arms quickly folded round her, pulling her close again, his lips meeting hers. When they separated, both of them were flushed, their eyes wide. Ellie could feel her heart hammering against her ribs. This was what she'd dreamt of. This was what she'd longed for since that moment on her birthday.

'What . . . what happened with Anna?' She forced the words out, but she had to ask.

'I finished with her. I had to. All the time I was with her these last few weeks I just kept thinking about you, trying to block you out, trying to stop thinking about you in that way, but it didn't work and . . .' He grinned suddenly. 'She is rather annoying. Do this. Do that.'

Ellie's eyes teased him. 'So you think *I* won't do that?'

'Oh, I'm sure you will,' Luke replied. 'Luckily, I like you a lot more than I liked her.' His expression grew more serious. 'What about Joe? I know you liked Joe once – are you sure you're really over him? And is he over you?'

'Oh, yes, so sure!' Ellie assured him. 'He's got a new girlfriend – well, someone he likes anyway.'

She saw the relief in Luke's eyes. 'I'm not like him. You and me – we'll fight. You know that.'

'But we'll make up. We'll make it work. Neither of us is the giving-up type.'

'Oh, I won't give up,' Luke said, and she saw the absolute conviction in his gaze. 'Not ever.'

'Nor me.' They stared at each other. *We're so alike*, she thought with a flash of clarity. *How can I not have seen it?* Luke stepped towards her and their lips met again. Briefly they were both lost in the moment, but finally Ellie pulled away. Her mind, her body, her heart were buzzing with happiness, but reality was slowly returning. 'There's something I have to do. Will you feed Hope and put her out in the field for me?'

'Sure.' Luke looked surprised. 'What is it?'

But Ellie shook her head. 'I can't tell you. Just something.'

'OK.' He touched her lips lightly. 'But come back soon.'

'I will,' she promised.

Ellie let herself in through the gate into Spirit's field. The breeze had dropped and the warm air was still. She walked up the slope, brushing away a fly that buzzed around her head and watching two white butterflies dancing over the grass. The warm weather had dried the earth on Spirit's grave even more and now it was the palest brown covered with thousands of flecks of green. Soon it would be grass all over. She glanced behind her and saw Len in one of the lower fields, talking to the horses, and Luke leading Hope out to be reunited with Gem. Life changed. It was true. Things always moved on.

Ellie remembered what she'd just said to Luke. She didn't give up easily, but she also knew that some battles couldn't be fought, some fights couldn't be won. This was one of them.

Walk in the present, she thought, gathering her courage.

She stopped by Spirit's grave and shut her eyes. *Spirit?*

I am here.

She felt his breath on her hands, sensed him standing in front of her. A hand seemed to squeeze her heart tighter and tighter. *Can we go into the woods? I need to be able to see you.*

Yes.

Ellie walked on up the field, feeling Spirit walking beside her quietly. She climbed the fence and he jumped over. Once in the privacy of the trees, he appeared to her, his body faint at first but gradually becoming solid. His eyes met hers, deep and dark as forest pools. She couldn't speak.

She put her arms round his neck.

Ellie? She heard his concern as he sensed her distress.

Spirit, I . . . I think we have to say goodbye.

She tensed, half scared of his reaction, but all she felt was a wave of overwhelming relief from him.

You're right. We do. I've been thinking about it for a while. I cannot stay any longer. You need to walk in your present and I need to walk in mine. They were the same, but they're different now. He nuzzled her shoulder.

Tears spilled out of Ellie's eyes and she hugged him as tightly as she could. But even though she was crying this goodbye didn't feel as it had when he'd been dying because this time, deep down, she knew it was the right thing to do. They had to set each other free.

Spirit breathed on her face, her hands, her arms. Ellie kissed him over and over, trying to fix the feel of him in her mind. She didn't dare ask the question in her mind. But Spirit read her thoughts.

Yes, we'll meet again. In another time and place, but for now this is goodbye. Use everything you have learnt. Help horses – heal them.

I will, Spirit, Ellie promised through her tears. *Always*. She stroked his face, his ears, his nose, filled with the impossibility of it all. There wasn't enough time. She wanted to stroke him forever. *You can't go.*

I must.

No!

Spirit lifted his muzzle to her face. His warm breath dried her tears and his love wrapped around her like a blanket. She hadn't thought it would be possible, but her anguish suddenly slipped away, leaving her calm and at peace. Even if he wasn't there with her, his love always would be. Nothing could change that. She swallowed and touched his face.

I love you. She meant it with every fibre of her being, every cell of her body. *I'll never forget you or forget what you've taught me.*

Good. Remember everything and smile. Spirit snorted and stepped away. Their eyes met one last time, a gaze of such intensity that Ellie would never forget it.

'Spirit . . .'

But he was gone. The place where he'd been standing was suddenly just an empty space in the trees.

Ellie waited for the pain to hit, but it didn't come. The feeling of peace stayed as her mind filled with thoughts of all the times she'd spent with him – grooming, riding, talking. The good times. They were what she remembered.

'I'll see you again one day, Spirit,' she whispered, and though her eyes prickled with tears, she smiled.

Luke was leaning against the gate that led into Gem and Hope's field, watching the little foal as she bucked around Gem, trying to make the older pony play. Ellie looked at Luke's long lean body and his dark hair curling at the nape of his neck, and felt the calm inside her give way to happiness.

'Hi,' she called.

He looked round. 'Hey there, you. Done what you needed to do?'

'Yep.'

Luke nodded to Hope. 'That foal is so cute. I can just see it now; you'll be stars of the show-jumping circuit. You'll thank me forever for saying you should buy her.'

'Oh, will I?' Ellie said. 'Well, maybe I'd have thought of the idea myself.'

'Nah,' said Luke, his blue eyes glinting teasingly. 'It's all down to me. I'm the one with the good ideas. Just accept it.'

Ellie shook her head. 'You are *so* arrogant!'

Luke grinned. 'But you love me?'

Oh, yes, Ellie thought simply. And, stepping into her future, she stepped into his arms.

On a Beach . . .

A white-grey horse stared across the deep blue sea. The land on the other side was calling to him, urging him to come. Taking one last look over his shoulder, he whinnied softly, his eyes full of love, and then he turned and plunged into the waiting waves . . .

With Special Thanks To . . .

The wonderful Julie Templeton and Fiona Wallace from the Julie Templeton Show Team for taking time out of their incredibly busy lives to talk to me and answer my endless questions about showing and for showing me around their amazing yard. Any mistakes or inaccuracies are entirely mine or down to artistic licence. May your ponies and riders reign supreme! To Marjorie and Tim at Lings Lane Riding Stables for their really useful thoughts and suggestions for other books in the Loving Spirit series. To Richard Cooper for all the great information on hospitals and intensive care wards. To Mark Yates and Sarah Dobbing for the first-hand account of an air-ambulance rescue. (All things in life come in useful, you see . . .) To my lovely editor, Alexandra Antscherl, for her input and enthusiasm. To my first readers, Lee Weatherly and Julie Sykes, for reassuring me and being such great, always-there friends. To all my other friends and to the people and horses in my life who inspired Ellie and Spirit's story. And most of all to Peter, for sending me away on two different occasions to haunted follies to write this book – it truly would not have been written without your endless patience, love and support. Thank you from the bottom of my heart!!